SONGLESS TUESDAY

& THE HEARTS OF POEMS UNWRITTEN

Names: Schermer, Realf, author.

Title: Songless Tuesday & the hearts of poems unwritten : a novel / Realf Schermer.

Description: Haworth, New Jersey : Angel 2C LLC, [2024]

Identifiers: ISBN: 979-8-9923119-2-1 (hardback) I 979-8-9923119-1-4 (paperback) I 979-8-9923119-0-7 (ebook) I LCCN: 2025900649

Subjects: LCSH: Loyalty--Fiction. I War--Social aspects--Fiction. I World War, 1914-1918--Fiction. I Resilience (Personality trait)--Fiction. I Hope--Fiction. I LCGFT: Romance fiction. I Historical fiction. I BISAC: FICTION / Romance / General. I FICTION / Historical / General.

Classification: LCC: PS3619.C3497 S66 2024 I DDC: 813/.6--dc23

SONGLESS TUESDAY

& THE HEARTS OF POEMS UNWRITTEN

a novel

REALF SCHERMER

ANGEL 2C LLC
HAWORTH, NEW JERSEY

To

Koryn, Clive, and Von

WET PAINT

IT WAS STOLEN, no - not taken - offered and accepted. Not in words, but expressed slowly in a glance, touch, embracing her in a shortness of breath.

A needed, soothing, almost painful touch followed with a tickle of a guilty heart. The first glance was gloss, gentle and clear. The mix of her eye color; brown, deep, almost black, expanded as she breathed, a million emotions seemed to collide as her fingers were drawn to the paint brushes that lay in front of her.

The tips of her fingers moved slowly across the wooden table covered in paint, her tiny hands revealing a unique vulnerable vocabulary. She moved with a misplaced awkwardness that was youthful and inviting, the handles of the brushes rattled as she fumbled them. Startled, she could feel herself about to blush, but the bristles on the brushes paused, silent, for just a moment as their hands touched.

A passing glance, moving inward, just to see her eyes, just as quickly to glance back, with the hope of not being noticed in a millisecond that felt like it lasted days. In that motion he imagined her facing him, her shoulders bare and her arms unfolded resting by her side. Her firm body positioned directly in front of him. Her right hand reached upward grazing the lower part of her smiling lips. When their eyes met the innocence of laughter would follow, making any inhibitions or shy feelings fade.

This was not hand-holding, her rich longing eyes said, "Find me!"

A blunt and quick-focused gaze landed directly on her quiet face. He would stare deeply as they talked, not blinking. She was seamless. Dimitri was enraptured, locked. He could see all. His focus and level of concentration was heightened. If he could look just a little deeper at the glossy reflection on her lips, he could understand how to replicate it on canvas. A brilliant highlight on the top edge of her right lip mirrored her eyes, specifically the point of light that made her iris sparkle. Instantly, it transitioned to shadow. Ruby in every tone, it was a range finding almost pink to a rich darkness stretching across her mouth. The sun's reflection found her lower lip in certain places leading to a deeper chiaroscuro. He couldn't see imperfection, a flaw never. He studied every detail of her form, beauty, and color.

He was caught in a paradox, admiring nature's little trick. So much is meant to be experienced and cherished rather than distilled and processed. He could spend a lifetime trying to figure out the combination of paint and technique to replicate her lips that were now indelibly written in his mind's canvas. It may not happen ever. Smiling, he thought it would be worth trying, over and over again.

"How close can I get," Dimitri said under his breath, "without chasing you away?"

"What?" Lily asked.

"I mean how close are you to Amelia?" Dimitri repeated.

"She is my oldest friend, a dear. I regard her and her family as my own, she really is like a big sister. She has been so supportive throughout my entire life. Amelia was the first of the debutantes to reject the litany of would-be suitors. She's strong willed, confident. I've tried to follow her example. I have two role models, Amelia and Marie, two of the most genuine souls I have ever met and their strength and compassion are unique and know no limits. I'm blessed that I know two women that possess these qualities. And they share them so generously with myself and others, like at the Servicemen Center."

"Amen," he affirmed.

"Amelia is a blessing - we have mutual hearts, she is also so respected and loved," Lily replied.

She had fond memories lying on the dock as Amelia would brush her hair and tell her what would likely happen next in school, at home and in their mutually pre-determined destiny. Lily's good fortune was delayed by her ex-husband's many issues; she was, however, fortunate, not to be outdone by those issues. Lily took a moment to try and determine who else in heart and life had supported her. She was thankful beyond measure for her other friend Marie, but she was nearest to Amelia in the love, support, and unending dedication to her.

"When I first met Amelia," Dimitri explained, "she spent the entire morning worrying about everyone else, all the boys. She has a generous soul."

"You only saw the surface, it really is her nature," Lily explained.

"I can't remember all of it, but the center certainly helped me, the expansion is going to reach a lot more of us. It's needed and necessary," Dimitri offered sincerely.

"When did you meet her?" Lily inquired.

"Twice, the first time was the Colonel's luncheon, then again, the week before the opening. I was happy to volunteer a little time and try to add some to the plate."

"Her mission is a big one, but I think if anything can get the community around a problem, it's her nature," Lily explained.

"She's going to help these fellas for years to come. The facility is gorgeous, state-of-the art! Made a real difference for me," Dimitri declared.

Lily looked at him and thought to herself something she could never say, but joyously wondered. Amelia was hoping to connect her and Dimitri, she mused. Amelia's craft and selflessness defined the intent behind a loving smile. She was at her best doing and helping others.

HE SURRENDERED

IT WOULD REQUIRE a proper introduction or a least a second look. A foundational establishment of trust initiating an early hint of chemistry that would move him just a little closer to his subject. Dimitri was usually safe when he told stories of his revered Aunt Renee who had raised him from a young boy. It was just enough of a personal outpouring that celebrated this important figure in his life, allowing whomever he was chatting with to understand her and his story. Of course, it was also about him, her piano, a love of music, and the melody he hears in his soul as he reminisces. Instantly, in a second breath, he gets back to the piano, peacefully. He remembers the music that made the exhausted collections of rooms in a small apartment, rich with passion and curiosity, a perfect home.

He was incapable of comprehending the determination it took to leave the town of Avignon where she was born and raised to immigrate to New York City. The struggles and despair that sighed in plazas beyond churches met grand stories of abundance and independence that motivated her. How did she make the cross-country trek to reach Roscoff? Did she borrow? Save? Share? Never steal. Was she part of a nomadic movement or did she step in solitude universally alone? Unsupported beyond a change of undergarments, a pair of sandals, and a worn jacket with a scarf inside a pocket, Renee remained determined. Once the vast ocean was in sight, looking westward she could sense an intangible sensation pulling her towards the water. How intrepid she was amid immeasurable uncertainty, possessing the grit to arrive virtually alone to start a new life, find community, and create a home. Her life in the tenement wasn't easy for a single woman. She worked six days a week and taught piano on Sunday afternoons. Dimitri had only vague memories of his parents. His mother passed away when he was very young due to a fever, and his father was always away "working." It was doubtful any consistent financial support reached Renee. She wasn't just a guardian or a caregiver, but rather a family in every way. Dimitri's world was rich with music, song, and immense love. A powerful counterbalance to the loss of his mother whose memory he could almost recall, and a father who was out of his life at an early age.

This was safe. He told Lily this was the deep well of passion that made him never tire when he painted. He could struggle to resist one more conversation, delaying yet again, what he was truly thinking as they spoke. He would keep his genuine feelings from her - that whenever he thought of her, regardless of what he was doing, he was lost, blissfully and completely lost.

Lily had more than a passing interest in music. During her school days she had performed in numerous theatrical productions to much acclaim. She started to hum the score to her former routine; melody filled her imagination instantly and she was transported back to first position.

The start of every new performance began with a magical eruption. Calm tension brewed by anticipation, extended throughout her body. Her legs were strong and lean. The sound of a light touch on a piano keyboard would rhythmically vault her to her toes, and the spirited visual art would gracefully begin, then rise. Across the sparse dimly lit stage the dance would swirl and build. She could feel her heart beating and would move instinctually, always keeping her breath measured and quiet. Practicing her routine, she was at peace. She could fill her mind with the music silently accompanying her.

It required discipline to be the lead dancer, an elusive distinction and title that she would never hold. She continued to practice her performance without music, soaked in the elation of the imagined live orchestra supporting melodic movements. Remembering well her dance and the highlights of her days as young performer, she started to experience the pains and tightness that were a part of graceful arms and limber legs. He saw movement, but felt her spirit. He wished she would study his face, chin and lips as closely and with the same degree of precision and intensity as he did when he focused on her. It wasn't a point of pressure talking with Lily; it was a natural peeling away of protective layers to reach a connection. A precious bond that revealed itself in its own unique way at a timing of its choosing. Dimitri was humbled just to be present when it arrived.

He could almost let his mind drift beyond the conversation. If he allowed himself to see her skin, would it be long enough to select the palette, the tone and color to accurately start the piece? This was anxiety and an important moment to question and review all creative choices. The painting held a specific purpose that was more significant than the commission that started the conversation. He was personally driven to do more, and at a higher level, an intimate and intense expression of love for Lily.

He surrendered with conversation. There was a silence, unmoved. In moments that stretched to minutes, the fateful feeling that he knew would be long lasting, fell. He found his breath. The world met again, he was repositioned in the light that filled the room. He imagined the tone and light joyously finding a composition with just the right depth. This would be a struggle, not of a masterpiece, he was too misplaced. Or maybe not. Too much distraction and worry. It would be an exhausting fight just to do justice to her beauty, his vision would have to wait.

"You will sit for me, of course?" Dimitri asked.

"Why?" She deflected with a smile.

He could only see her face. The rest of the room was a blur as he tried to slow his breath. Instantly, he could envision the perfect body position, not just sketched, but applied in rich color, with highlights swirling in tiny strokes along her brown auburn hair. This startled him, and it gave him the excited confidence sometimes enjoyed by fully engaged artists. He would remind himself that with each new endeavor, this confidence fades, falling to revision and second-guessing, and the betraying need to please others.

"It's easy, won't hurt, even a little," he chuckled.

His head faced the floor as his eyes reached upward. He hoped she would sense his sincerity. His ear could only hear himself hoping to remain calm, slowing his breathing. He managed small talk and stepped closer.

The echo of a city, usually full of loud, was sinisterly quiet as her gaze touched the high ceiling windows in the studio. It was an afternoon of intrigue. She had stayed too long and was concerned it made her unable to say anything other than yes. And even with their conversation of small syllables, she felt radiant and warm. She knew this was the only place she could imagine herself, at least for the time being.

Through a tall window she could see a fast-moving dark cloud engulfing every ounce of light that could squeeze through the glass. The deep staccato sound of oversized summer raindrops followed.

For Dimitri, this was the solution. The lights lowered, brought down by nature and a muted sky. This was a bit painterly and indeed, artful, defiant, but resourceful. Just a kiss of light falling through the narrow, tall window would touch her face. He felt the mystery that came with the shape of the light. It was more a unique quality of light, never the amount - the portrait was in his sights. He could truly breathe easier now. He could manage the rest in between.

As the clouds rolled past, a strong ray of light streaked across the city, beaming through the windows. It was the warm color she noticed first. The heat-lifted breeze that flew into the studio moved the edge of her white dress. She was quick not to allow an immodest moment. The gust of air filled the space with a soothing squall that was urgent and refreshing.

HE KNEW

H E KNEW HER. She made him feel half his age, and
indeed ageless. He imagined they were lifelong friends,
children who chased each other across the field, on long
summer evenings that never really end.

Even the steady scratch of the stiff grass under his bare
feet as he followed her across the lawn wouldn't dampen
his growing excitement. He could hear her laugh and hear
her breathe as they sprinted toward the water. Running,
she looked back at him over her shoulder, they were just
a step apart at full stride. He could see the green hue of a
necklace floating just off her skin, bouncing and bouncing,
without ever touching her chest, or resting still.

Warmth surrounded her body as her dress took flight,
flowing angelically in the breeze. The day's end brought a
bound of energy, bursting them from their formation. He
would never catch her, even as she reached her hand out
to him. She was aloft, her feet seeming never to touch the
ground. She turned smoothly and swiftly; her quick steps
flowed quietly. He couldn't reach her, but he knew she
would never leave him.

It made sense in another daydream. Twenty years
or so had passed and this fast and elusive running pair
stood together in the field. Lily's skin was tan, she wore

an infatuating smile. Her white gown sparkled, catching highlights of the sun, as she moved. He noticed her short sleeves showcasing the length and grace of her arms. Around her neck she wore a long strand of white and colorful stones, gems, and pearls, tied with a purple line of silk. The Athenian style of her hair held auburn curls adorned with small white wildflower blossoms, woven with two ribbons, one ivory the other a soft green. When she spoke her words were true, a comforting short giggle followed, bringing a universal and playful sense of unity to the assembled group.

The grass was higher today, as Dimitri stretched his arm out. As she turned, he could see her gloved fingers were holding a small bouquet, a handhold of collected flowers, light as air. Her movements were slight, she was delicate, but full of energy. Dimitri couldn't look away. As firmly as she stood, he could sense how fragile, indeed precious she was, in between another flashing smile. In a glance, a powerful message of commitment radiated affectionately from the depths of her soul, making it clear to him that she was ready to take ownership of every success and failure that they would ever face in an unscripted relationship destined to flourish amid the thunder and flash of passion's chaos.

Dimitri felt jubilant, his hopeful outlook upheld by the smiling faces of his family and friends. Some who had parted, and others who had fallen in action, could they see him? Could they sense his sincerity and the reverence that he held for each one of them? It was humility that welled the limits of his emotions filling his heart with memories adorned with affection.

He blinked his eyes and came out of it.

Shaking his head he exhaled an endless breath. His resting hand gripped the chair in front of him for balance as he wiped the sweat and tears from his face. He wondered how he could find this sunset meadow, the one with the light just right. He wondered how he could find - no create - this matrimonial union. Was he ready? Reaching for another bottle, he toasted to his wish to be with Lily, renewing a commitment to reach the meadow, feel the sunshine, surrounded by the blessings and love of his family and his friends.

He took a second swig from the green bottle.

QUIET MOMENTS

I N QUIET MOMENTS, she felt stared at, in a manner that made her body tingle and blush. It began slowly as the color of her face shifted from a soft to a brilliant ruby red. Fighting to catch her breath, and maintain the mystery of their mutual longing, she would start to look away. Above his canvas on a shelf, the yellow lush color of three Mexican ornaments caught her eye. Shiny, flat, tin, pressed metal shapes sat next to the small gilded ornamental clock that no longer functioned. Standing higher on the shelf was a collection of worn, well-used funnels whose metals had started to rust and had developed gentle hues of faded color. It was a curious collection of material, textures, and shapes, and she couldn't wait to ask. Were these items a distracted tray of bric-a-brac to move words in labored conversations?

Never would he reveal what they were for and the role they played in his work. Sadly, his collection of found and eclectic items was growing.

"You like them?" Dimitri asked.

"O' yes!" She offered, surprised he noticed her distraction, "how did you find such a random assortment of such interesting things? I love the color of the yellow one."

"For a time, I was a collector of vintage toys; however,

I wouldn't consider myself to have the discerning eye that you do," Dimitri said.

He kept some toys, gifts from his aunt. He offered few words, not wishing to rob from concentration.

He winced as he felt the depth of his lie, not to her, but to himself. This pained his ears as his lips uttered the words. Each piece was a walk to a market, a trip, a subtle or vibrant tool to take his mind to a new surrounding of color or light – to move his senses, a connection to a more advanced track in the process. He wouldn't even look at the collection, he liked where he was at the moment. He used the items to break out of "artist's block." They could delete the painful and harsh stalling of creativity, which fuels limitless doubt and self-exiling fear.

Each item handled the shadow, shape and intensity of light in a unique manner. Raising the level of questioning – taking his work to a place not of joy alone, but revealed as studied with a hint of sophistication.

He worried, as he was in an approach that did justice to what he wanted, he wouldn't want that to change or to use a revisionist eye. This would start safely to remove all notions of risk. He progressed to intentional movements, but he had been here before; each a layer on a prior block, or coming from a directed stroke. This would change his senses just enough to allow an idea to evolve, flourish or fade.

Dimitri's love for Lily was joyous, rich in his heart, but he couldn't say it out loud - he wouldn't tell her, not yet. This didn't need to be perfect, but it was early, unrefined, cherished, but raw. He used the conflict of his evolving emotions as he painted. His brush strokes would tickle his body with a self-indulgent chill making him either stay in between lines, or surrender creativity and unchain his affections. He wondered if he put too much thought into the items on the shelf, would his vision change? Would his approach have to follow?

The weeks passed, one following another. His confidence was elevated. He was, by any measure, cocky. Lily's portrait was among his best, a cherished piece he would hate to part with, but taking solace knowing she would have it.

"Would she?" he murmured to himself in a whisper.

Dimitri knew her giving and generous nature allowed his work to end up anywhere or worse. The painting was marked by a unique use of mixing colors in a manner that was innovative and exciting. He relied heavily on the most dramatic gray, black and highlights. He mixed vibrant yellows and hues of red with gentle strokes to adorn the brim of an oversized white hat detailed with a thin silver trim.

Each stroke emboldened the last, the color searing far beyond the canvas. For Dimitri this was meaningful, blissful, and right.

He committed to a vista, a mountain view of dramatic scale with her body dressed in black, marching uphill on a path heading toward a landing, on the right third of the canvas. The scene went on to infinity; below her he placed a lush valley with an orchard nestled near a narrow winding waterway. Her body position was commanding, her countenance was full of life. Her bright large eyes and lips seduced the senses and could not be avoided. A halo created by a horseman's hat glowed, surrounding her hair. It was strung off the shoulder with a lariat draped around her neck resting above the open collar of a white blouse. Her right hand held a single wildflower, her left hand rested on a black leather belt that held a rope and a small silver-handled dagger.

It was the touch of a skilled artist and in a different

year, a widely held perspective would describe their kiss and this painting, as a masterpiece. This was something unlike his other attempts. The collection of gathered paint that gummed the bristles in the hair of his brushes, every color and no color, were gone. Each stroke was clean, true, artful and loving. In the oversized work he took great pains to balance her gentle nature with the self-reliant strength that she newly discovered.

He could relax in conflict. A paused studio pained him. He could feel every degree of temperature rising as the sun warmed the room. His cupboard was stocked, but it bored him, the gin was not crisp, and left a wax coating layering his tongue. Every idea held a locked medley, with a thick consistency in need of a churn; unmet or without a voice or challenge, it would start to rot. This emotionless drain and defeatism would fill another day with hours of waiting, surrounded by strands of ideas, fighting for inspiration. The elasticity of stretched seconds expanded, intentionally unwilling to tick past another hopeless moment. He would see Lily in three days, just enough time to worry, long enough to create dreams, reimagine those dreams, and hope for a spark of chemistry.

If she were to walk in alone, he would use his easel to display the now well-curated piece. He would see her quietly from the corner room seated, he would wait for her to arrive. She knew the way in and rushed eagerly to the door. Two glowing streaks were the only points of light that were visible. Dimitri took great joy in noticing that the painting was staged, positioned just so, held in a dramatic lighting. He had placed the canvas in a modest wood frame painted a dark deep blue, the edge and trim, a radiant gold. Sparkle and shadows.

RIGHT NOW

S HE SMILED WHEN she heard his footsteps. He moved slowly as he walked towards her. He was a welcoming host who helped remove her wet coat and hung it where it could dry. He held her hand as he walked her into the main space of his studio.

She was instantly overcome by her likeness on the canvas. To him it was more than just another piece, but it was breathtaking to Lily. This was a glowing tribute of ageless art that would hold her youth, beauty, and grace forever. Her body shivered with a fever of racing emotions. Did she reveal too much? No, it was perfect! She turned exuberantly.

The embrace came naturally. First he drew her closer under his arm as she made the turn towards him. With one glance he saw a tear in her eyes, her lips, her breasts; he noticed the lace embroidery gracing her neck. As she raised her chin a thin shadow of lace fell across her neck and disappeared.

He looked at her for one last time, gazing deeply into her eyes, moving down to her lips, and back to the center of her pupil. As they stood closer together, he lightly touched the brooch on her jacket. She smiled; it was her favorite piece of jewelry. The emerald glass sparkled as she moved nearer to the light coming in through the window. The sea glass was positioned like the petals of a flower. He stepped closer. Lily lowered her chin, attempting to hide the fact that she was fully blushing.

Their first kiss was an awakening, an initiating milestone, heartening an already strong connection. The second kiss brought a liberating sense of abandonment. Their hands and arms locked and were immediately electrified. She was surrounded by him - all of him. Lily couldn't remember the last time her heart pounded this way. She felt herself start to glisten with moisture, wet with a gentle sweat. Patient movements, she giggled softly as his strong hands guided her across the hall to a small room with a tiny square window above a long sofa.

"But wait, no wait, oh no…no, don't stop!" She gasped, moving her hand through his hair.

They kissed again.

The intoxicating scent of her perfume rose from the couch and sent a message of innocence that was fresh and inviting, captivating Dimitri. His sensitive nature was the outlier portion of a well-built, military-trained lieutenant. Right now, his focus had urgently shifted to only things physical. Lily moved her hands from his neck to the muscles across his broad shoulders feeling how exquisitely firm and strong he was to the touch. His skin was ablaze and warm to her lips as she kissed his chest gently. Lily worked on the laces of her silk corset, as the light afternoon rain continued to fall. They once again pulled apart, a post-embrace reset; a renewed transformation to find each other with a clear purpose. Dimitri stroked her legs. First a chuckle, next a kiss. Now the pair were free to be more daring and they found an exuberance in their athletics which would be shared for hours. Dimitri didn't understand the powerful energy they felt when they first met, but it was a chemistry that guided them here. He would respect it, matching drive with determination.

Lily's coy unavailability disappeared amidst a new and complete rapture, a commitment she knew had more than slight consequences. She commanded herself in body, mind, and soul to fight off the elation of the moment. A losing effort, forcing an irrational tension between all things proper and that which she knew to be love or lust, but had never allowed herself to fully and delightfully surrender. What would be the price of an emotional contest, she thought, just random folly? She remembered what others had almost done and described with embellished detail later, over luncheons she would seldom miss and always swear off.

Not a taste – something familiar, not sure she would have gone back to – ever. A wider smile, a powerful foot pedaling, as the lovers moved. With both arms outstretched, Lily gasped a series of quick short breaths. She held firmly to the edge of the sofa's fabric to stabilize her body, and clenched her teeth as her legs began to shake in a rhythmic way that was powerfully unbridled.

Dimitri's enormous hand rested firmly on her lower back, supporting her and guiding her in direction and tempo. Her fragrance danced lightly in the air, covering the soft cushions. Dimitri smiled, as the pair whispered words of approval and instruction in half spoken syllables. He would rest easy in the nights that followed, clinging to pillows covered in her scent and dreaming of the accelerated staccato of their private language.

In the conflict between what she wanted and what had happened, she was an enthusiastic lover who wished to remain independent. A willingness to be held in a blissful serenade, she questioned herself trying to find a piece of a confident chuckle. Escape to wine, one day, she thought. Touch, this was not surrender, an embrace, love? O' god, she wondered, lying back down. This! What to do?

"My sweet, my word!"

She was smiling, lost in self-deprecating elation, and then humanity called her back. Electric silence followed, then sleep.

ORCHID TIME

THE SCARCELY-FILLED passenger car left plenty of room to spread out and get comfortable. Dimitri preferred the quiet of the rear cars and the opportunity to look out from the door of the last car. A large duffel bag with bundles of food wrapped in different papers filled one seat directly across from them. They packed enough clothes and sturdy hats to brave the sun, wind, and surf for the short getaway. The journey from Grand Central Station to Babylon was just long enough for one to get comfortable, have a sandwich, and share a sip or two from a discreet flask. The trek out to the island was always made measurably shorter when accompanied by his vibrant and attractive travel companion.

Riding the train always felt exotic, regardless of how hot, steamy or loud it could be at times. The window let in a refreshing flow of air, cooling their skin. Lily enjoyed the view seeing the communities and towns zip past. In an instant, each told a textured story, allowing her mind to reflect on the lives of people she saw in the blink of another glance. Lily's wardrobe reflected an elegant athletic look; a light white dress with an open neck that fell past her knee landing on her shin. She wore a tan belt around her waist with a light summer blazer, and on her head a black scarf with yellow details that held up the different layers of her hair. Dimitri placed his hand on her soft neck to pull her to him, he kissed her gently, as she rested on his chest. He playfully teased her hair, a fashionable style on which she'd spent close to an hour to get it to look the way she'd hoped.

He wondered how her wardrobe would change as they got closer and closer to their destination. The rhythm of the train lulled the pair to the edge of sleep only to be interrupted by the whistle of an oncoming train.

His sturdy embrace held her as she curled her body tighter under his arms. Dimitri gently touched her leg as they approached the station. As she opened her eyes, he started to gather their bags.

"I promised you deep relaxation," Dimitri said smiling, "and now we're moments away."

He had a number of things to carry, and took a second to get organized, placing a package of food tied with a string at the top of the pile.

"I'll carry that one," Lily offered.

"No, it's important to keep your lovely hands free, and for you to hold my hand," he said with a smile.

Lily understood that he wasn't meaning to treat her like child, he was being protective of her. Her eyebrows shrugged with concern, but she took comfort later, knowing how deeply he cared. Walking down the platform steps of the station, the couple would have a short walk from the village green to a small pier at the bottom of a steep cobblestoned hill.

The sounds changed as they got closer to the dock. Workers in denim overalls raced and swirled around filling small boats, and slightly larger ones with more and more crates. Fresh fish was being off-loaded, displayed, sold, and carried off in carts. Voices were raised and random pieces of ice lay scattered in their path. This was more industrial then Lily's normal mode of transportation. Everything she saw, heard or smelled around her was new, moving fast. She was intrigued.

"Stephen!" shouted Dimitri.

"So, this is her!? Brilliant! Hello! Now I get it!" Stephen loudly questioned knowing the answers. He was beaming.

The two men hugged, and their shared bond was clear and powerful. Stephen was a smaller, thinner, and slightly tanner version of Dimitri. He was youthful, handsome, and led with affection and a radiant smile.

"This is Stephen, he's the best," Dimitri said proudly, presenting his lifelong friend to Lily.

"Pleasure to meet you!" Lily bubbled.

Stephen wore thick khaki trousers tied with a long strand of leather that circled his waist numerous times and was locked in place by an ornate sailors knot that relaxed hanging to his thigh. His moccasins were worn. His shirt was a faded gray, an afterthought of a t-shirt with his bulky arms dominating the sleeve.

"It's been too long! How are you?!" Dimitri asked, resting his hand on his buddy's shoulder.

The two shouted back and forth as Stephen moved across the entire boat. They both talked at the same time, like small children laughing and finishing each other's thoughts. It was refreshing to see such a joyful reunion.

"Step aboard and watch the line," Stephen warned.

The boat was too small to be a ferry, but it was a vessel he could move along the coast, without causing a stir.

The rocking of the boat felt strange to Lily, who kept her palm open and near her shoulder ready to grab a railing if needed.

Dimitri shouted, "Captain!" to Stephen with a smile, tossing the wrapped package of cheese and dried goods tied with a string.

"No, much too generous, and always not necessary."

Dimitri knew all of Stephen's favorites, including cash. Great cured meats, cheese, and food of every type that were easily found in Dimitri's neighborhood, but elusive and harder for Stephen to find on the water.

The next offering was a bottle of wine.

"I'm told it's a good vintage," Dimitri explained. "Let's open it and share it together over the holidays."

The idea of spending a holiday apart would never be entertained and at minimum would be considered a brotherly betrayal.

Just as Dimitri placed the package on the cushion of the seat, Lily lost her step and reached out as she fell toward Dimitri. He smiled as he caught her.

"That's why I asked you to keep your hands free."

Dimitri used this as an opportunity to hold Lily against his body for a brief hug. She pecked his check, ever playful.

Stephen stood on a raised platform and asked Lily to stand with him.

"Hold this," he asked.

He instructed Lily to take the wheel. She had never been on the working end of an actual fishing boat. Lily smiled. She enjoyed being trusted and brought in to participate. Stephen rolled a smoke and offered it to her. Lighting up, he took time to slowly admire Lily from head to toe, as he exhaled.

"Aim for those large hills just at the horizon on the starboard side. How long have you known Dimitri?"

Stephen asked.

"I think a little, well, a month or so, more, I would guess," she said stumbling over her reply.

It wasn't a matter of time or days. Her first memory at the studio was a flash of a single bare stem of an orchid plant seated on a low shelf near a thin window. Yesterday, the orchid was in bloom, with three ample white blossoms on each side.

"We met three, no six blossoms ago!" She chuckled loudly, "In orchid time." Her body shook with exuberance.

"Apologies, I don't mean to be out of turn. Dimitri knew my brother, they even fought together in the war. We're sort of the only family each other have. I hope you didn't think I was prying," he explained, a bit embarrassed.

After a slight pause, he smiled and confessed, "I was."

They shared a laugh and Lily very generously gave him a pass. She hadn't kept track of how long they were together. Was it a few weeks or months? Or was it an entire season? She would celebrate the richness of their relationship no matter how short or long of a time it lasted.

"I would say just over a few months, but it feels as passionate as the instant we first met," she offered.

Lily felt a wave of confidence having expressed her commitment to Dimitri out loud for the first time. She bent her body toward the wheel, bending low from the hips. She extended her long legs firmly in a wide stance. Here, she stretched her back moving lower and rocking right and left to release the tension in her strong slender legs. After a wide-eyed stare that revealed all of her perfect ass and athletic frame, Stephen quickly turned away out of respect for his friend.

The rhythm of the boat's movement quieted the conversation, and Lily could feel the boat gliding over the waves lulling her into a peaceful trance.

In a few minutes, Stephen started to bark orders as the boat moved closer to a dock right in front of them. Dimitri shouldered all of the bags and looked at Lily.

"Keep your hands free, he's not stopping this thing," he said.

"What?!"

"We just step onto the dock – watch your hands and feet," he warned.

Lily stepped with Dimitri following his lead, his hand guiding her off the boat resting lightly around her waist. Stephen was still speaking loudly as he waved at Lily and shouted,

"I will find you in a few, ENJOY!"

As the motor sputtered away, soft quiet filled the air; the sounds were like music, steady and enchanting. The tiny waves of the bay rhythmically seeped through the rocks, looking for sand, over and over again.

"You knew Stephen's brother, yes?" Lily asked.

"For years, my whole life, in the army too. We were sent to France together. Eli was my closest friend, he is missed greatly, but his passing has brought us closer together, in a good way."

"What you have is special, he loves you," Lily admired. "What does he do? He does indeed seem busy."

Dimitri took a second, he could trust Lily empirically, but it was a subject he almost never discussed.

"Stephen's life is the water, always has been since he was a little boy. He knows every cove, river, sandbar, and inlet from Orient Point to Atlantic City, just about. He's part of a tight community of those who have a deep love for the ocean, and make their living from it. They understand all of the complexities of life on the sea and respect it. When we're together on land Stephen looks up to me, but on the water, he's the Captain. After the war, Stephen was doing minor shipping with a few small boats, not really using the regular customs channels, if you know what I mean. Prohibition made him, and made him the first taste of real money he'd ever possessed. He had teams of small fishing boats in place, moving every type of spirit or wine from all over Canada, Great Britain and the Caribbean. Stephen oversees the thin islands over the bay to a deeper ocean. South of us beyond Sandy Hook his old friend Piero is in control, and thankfully he loves Stephen like a son." Dimitri explained.

"That's so lovely, just like a son," Lily repeated, finding this enterprise, as Dimitri was describing it, to be unique.

"The intercoastal channels belong to Pinco Cheng, and lucky for Stephen his trade covers a full range of illicit offerings, all except liquor. I've never met them, but with the support of trusted friends and family, they built a regional alliance. They're busy. His associates go beyond being friendly competitors; they're a work family. I mean why fight? They have a strong alliance not just for mutual prosperity, but for survival. It's about control and managing a space. Stephen can't cover as much alone, and by working together, they secure the region. With them and the help of a few cousins and a few more in Ireland, they control an intricate market all the way to Cape May.

His edge is that he has friends, and he's loved. He respects the "big fish" who thinks he's valuable, and he's considerate of others and their needs. I helped him with some capital, money I saved from the Army and then found a few other sources of income for him. The bay is an economy based on trade, products, transport, discretion, money, and favors. The undercurrent is trust. The rub is you can't have too many outstanding debts. If you owe too many favors, others will refuse you when you're in need. That's why I've always had his back," he continued.

"Over the years his contacts grew, as did his partnerships. Stephen knows every officer, sailor, dockworker and they all believe in him. I live at the studio. Stephen keeps a few autos there. But, my buildings make me whole, they bring in a solid income. With Stephen my participation is really like a silent investor. Enough talk, let's get you changed, and settled in."

"How will he know when we are ready to leave?"

"Leave? That small rope at the end of the dock holds a trap, we just tie the knot to the opposite pillar near the top, and it will signal him. He travels by a few times a week."

As they started down a long narrow path of fine sand, Dimitri suggested to Lily that she take off her shoes. "The sand isn't so hot." On both sides were low cactus plants and taller sea grass that stretched to a hill full of trees and bushes. This was a barrier island and it looked deserted.

"Are we alone?" Lily wondered

"No, well kinda, watch your step!" he warned.

"HEY," Lily jumped, "that tickled."

The tail of a large white cat graced Lily's ankle.

"Alone?"

"He lives here too, I call him Gibson," Dimitri told her with a smile.

"It was the name of the liquor I was enjoying when I found him, or he found me."

Lily took one look at Gibson and said, "That beauty may be a Greta, have you ever checked?" noting the piercing hazel eyes.

"I've never gotten close enough, but look at him. He's got the solid steel chin of a patrol sergeant, and the concentration of an artist, look at that stare! Tell you what, let's call him G.G. till we know for certain."

"Perfect. Hello, angel!"

Lily watched G.G. dart down the edge of the path, finding anything other than sand to walk on. She followed and Dimitri walked behind her. The pace slowed as they started walking up a slight incline. Lily got a more complete answer to her question as they approached the top of the dune, as she looked south, east, and west - she could see different levels of the island. They were isolated, and delightfully alone. The ocean air flowed through her hair, a hint of sea salt found her lips. The sand under her feet gave warmth as the prevailing winds raced off the ocean soothing her body and clearing her mind. She was soulfully relaxed and excited by everything she could see or discover.

A moment later she could see the red terracotta roof of a small beach bungalow. Getting closer, the sound of the ocean waves crashing on the beach became more pronounced and the forcefulness of it made her giddy.

"This is truly lovely, and so unique, how did you find it? Did you rent it?" she asked.

Dimitri told Lily the long version of the story, that lasted until he placed their belongings on the collection of chairs on the small patio of the cottage.

The property once belonged to Eli, Stephen's brother, from the inheritance of an old fisherman who was a distant uncle. It passed to Stephen who found himself in the heart of a business reversal and needed quick funds. It was important to Stephen to keep the cottage close and he asked Dimitri to take a partial share in the house. Ironically, the location was shared by both of them anyway. Dimitri had the money, and was more than happy to help his younger friend.

The second time Stephen needed money, Dimitri did the same and now owned the cottage outright.

"Don't be concerned, he is always welcome and at home here, but will never show up uninvited if I have a guest here."

The unlocked door opened to an unremarkable main room. Candles, books, a single trumpet, and a guitar were placed on a low bookcase on the western wall.

"So many books!" she exclaimed heading quickly into the room.

The northern wall across from the door held one of Dimitri's paintings, a landscape of the sand and sea with a sunset in a ruby and steel etched sky. Stuck in the frame was a small black and white photo of the two friends in uniform, hugging during a celebration. The wall connected to the door had a fireplace, a sofa with two chairs facing the door. Across from the door was a small kitchen, and to the left of the painting another door to a bedroom.

Through the bedroom was a small bathroom with a sink and toilet; lit sporadically with electricity, an extravagant addition that Stephen took great pains to make happen, given the remote location. Next to the bed were two small tables, and a Franklin sewing machine in need of a thoughtful operator and a repair.

Three large worn straw hats hung on wood pegs, next to two fishing poles on the right of the door. In the left corner of the main room, next to the fireplace, was a small lantern on top of a collection of books with birds on the cover. Sheets of paper were stuck among the pages. There was a fan on the ceiling and each wall had two windows.

Under the table Lily noticed three small barrels.

"Those are full of wine," he smiled. "There is plenty of liquor behind the wall of the cabinet across from the sink."

Her toe noted the slight incline of the floor pitching eastward. A subtle reminder of the need for constant upkeep at the cottage, a low priority given the day's new adventure. Dimitri was well aware that nothing in the house was square or level and he fully appreciated when a window or door closed completely. The chimney stood straight reaching toward the sky, aimed directly toward the north star. Lily leaned her shoulder against the doorframe and continued to take in more of her detailed observation.

A soft purr caught her ear. She noticed G.G. resting, nestled in the corner of the windowsill, clearly in command cradled in the embrace of the refreshing breeze rolling off the ocean. Without moving his head or blinking his eyes G.G. seemed to be counting and tracking each wave, as if to monitor performance and ensure its timely arrival.

Emerging from the bedroom, Dimitri stood facing Lily in the bottom half of a light cotton union suit, with torn pant legs, shortened to the knee.

"I'm going to check on the traps and see what might be on the menu for later. You should change and remember, no one is here, please be comfortable, it can get hot. Grab a hat by the door!"

Lily took that to heart finding a light sheer brassiere that laced on the sides for a top with matching bloomers that covered her waist to her knees. This was certainly not something she'd be seen wearing in public.

Dimitri grabbed the long wooden-handled rake from the back of the cottage, placed a weathered sun fedora on his head, and headed toward the bay. Lily was alone for a few minutes and reflected on how energized and alive this little cottage made her feel. It was the stark simplicity, the opposite of how she had traveled and vacationed in years past that made her feel at ease and happy for the first time in a long time. She wondered for a moment about the future, and being with Dimitri. It felt powerfully sincere, even if she didn't have a complete handle on their relationship.

Staying at the beach she decided to intently focus on the two of them, immersing herself in this joyous new adventure. Her mind was boldly clearing out the distracting scars of pain and drama that had muted her positive outlook for too long. She felt an easy sense of renewal taking hold in her body. The breeze that surrounded the cottage was a powerful potion, a restorative elixir that enveloped her with a new feeling of optimism. This transformation took personal strength and understanding, it was an inspiring new beginning for Lily.

All it took to put so much in the past, was to dare to find love, but more importantly, to allow oneself the openness to connect to love in a more meaningful way. Her feelings of appreciation and gratitude led to a smile as she looked around the modest bungalow. She exhaled and felt genuinely blessed that she boarded a taxi, took a train, a walk, a ferry-ride, and befriended a mighty white cat, to discover a new starting point that was emotionally vibrant and full of hope.

DIE NACHT

DIMITRI LEARNED QUICKLY that to stay alive in the Argonne, he had to keep moving. Swiftly! With urgency he navigated the labyrinth of support trenches surrounded by the screeching sounds of death and the pleas of the dying; he did his best to ignore it, not hear it or see it. Wounded men looking for assistance and solace lined the deep muddy corridor looking for a smoke as he brushed by them. The smell of burning flesh was ever-present, and the oscillating hell of corrosive air was unbreathable. The sound of gunfire and explosions was relentless, often accompanied by the screams of those facing a bullet and sometimes their haunting last breaths.

Eli and Dimitri understood that to pause, stop, or join in assisting others in any capacity, was the first step in being volunteered for something beyond unimaginable terror. He had been there before; catching his breath for only a few seconds. Dimitri faced orders that shortly had him racing towards a rain of gunfire. He could feel their velocity as the bullets traced his ears. These were moments of bayonets, surrounded by German screams. No one could really hear voices. Screams, which then became faded whispers of pain, were everywhere, far off, and faint. Only the volume of explosions and the presence of fire and gas, got anyone's undivided attention. Dimitri's thoughts lingered on the idea of having permanent hearing damage, but given his current environment, it was low on his list of concerns.

Even then, one had to be able to walk and talk all at once. Try to survive and try to kill, hoping to save another from a worse fate while praying to make it through just one more day, and one step closer to home.

"Kill, Death, Die. Kill, Death, Die. KDD. KDD," he repeated. The heart-stopping sounds of gunfire that he felt in uncontrollable twitches over and over.

Eli and Dimitri had served on the front and in forest trenches. Both had specific roles. Dimitri was a courier who carried classified information, quickly and discreetly, between forces that were unable to make contact.

Dimitri never disobeyed orders, or ignored the chain of command, but he knew his directives and followed them without fail. Avoiding his fellow solders upon arrival in a combat area was often the best way to prevent the questioning and wasteful approvals needed to reach command. The last hundred yards of a mission could be as troubling as a cross-country trek. He took a direct approach marching face-to-face to the officer he was instructed to serve with a dispatch. Often, his interaction with command led to a description of everything he had seen or heard along his journey. He would get dismissed with, "Very good," or "That is all," and occasionally given a letter in reply. In all cases he left with the same urgency. Dimitri attempted to piece together what was being described in the dispatches. He could discern the tone of the messages by looking at the body language or facial expressions of the intended recipient, invariably resulting in a crumpled dispatch tossed in anger in the direction of another officer in the headquarters.

Dimitri marched as fast as he could past new arrivals, a group of thirty men who would spend the next three days fighting to stay alive in a cold, dark, wet front-line trench. One bullet and one scream away from the hands of the enemy.

Mud covered his boots and the cuffs of his pants. His uniform wasn't especially unique, he made it his own and it served him well. His leather gas mask was a luxury, an upgrade from a urine-drenched handkerchief, it rested next to a small pouch of ammunition that stood ready in support of his Colt 1911. He used it often, each time bringing terror and an awful memory of a tragic KDD nightmare set to repeat and recoil. Three lethal knives fit snugly in his waistband helping to define his arsenal; one was a sturdy handled combat knife, the other two were smaller throwing blades; each had saved his life, simultaneously ridding the universe of another cursed soul. In solitude he shouted, then held his tongue, unclear how to respond to himself or reset his death-soaked mental state. He wondered what quantitative tool he could use to measure and properly access his own barbaric bloodlust. He spent hours in formation, then alone, seeking a soothing or blunt antidote. He wished for half a distraction. In the fresh air beyond the explosions he silently offered another prayer. He was humble and felt gratitude.

He relished the smell of the lush forest away from the action. In the dark vast Argonne, his keen instincts taught him not to disrupt and to be aware enough to survive and not succumb to the uncaring laws of natural selection. The carnage and cries of death far from the eyes of civilization lived unheard in the continuum of trails and unblown winds. One next to the other, enormous oaks, uprooted, resting on its neighbor. A full-sized fallen tree suspended in mid-flight, remarkably unfinished and precarious enough to be an avoidable peril.

In a perfect world, one rode by train or transport to travel the hilly countryside. He had to be more inventive. Dimitri was often ferried by civilians; he had the innate ability to make trusted connections when needed. He always kept moving. Without a letter or instruction, he had standing orders to return to his post, currently outside Verdon. His post's location fluctuated mirroring the movement of the front. Here, one Major, his command, oversaw scores of couriers, whose reach covered the region. Otherwise, he was on his own and thrived doing his job having to report to no one for most of his service.

His role afforded him access to water and meals with greater certainty, and better quality than most soldiers could expect. He used his rations as currency on the road, for a safe place to rest, or a better cut of cheese.

It was a bustling muddy road outside the town where he first saw the lovely Fabienne. Dimitri leaped out of the small wagon that ferried him to help her. She was spinning, struggling with her arms full of parcels and a small child she attempted to keep in front of her.

"Let me help you with those," he offered.

"Merci, je m'appelle Fabienne. Very kind of you."

"I'm Dimitri," he said, as he handled the parcels with ease and made a fast friend with the young boy. With her hands free Fabienne closed her cloak and buttoned the collar across her neck. Dimitri had traveled this stretch of road numerous times and had never seen her before.

"It will be a great relief to be off this dirt road, especially with Henri. He's so busy and loves seeing all the loud trucks and equipment," she said, as she gave the boy a smile.

They turned off the road and started a trek taking just under half an hour, walking on long empty dirt roads. Strained at first, the conversation led this new acquaintance to sense the trusting nature of her American companion. She could finally face him with a smile. Fabienne had lost her husband to the war, and as a single woman had an overload of misplaced attention and advances from lonely soldiers. He enjoyed the graceful accent of her soft voice. Her son had found his way to Dimitri's shoulders, and the mom laughed as the young boy covered his eyes. It was clear there was not an abundance of joyous happenings in which the child could take part.

Turning to face a setting sun, Fabienne led them down a short lane reaching a low fence that encased a small front yard complementing two modest homes. A chicken stood on the step of the first cottage, but the smoke flowing from the chimney of the one on the far edge of the yard left Dimitri confused.

"Forgive me, I thought you were alone here. I didn't mean to trespass into a courtship?"

"Nonsense, that is my aunt's home. We live over here," she said pointing to the door next to the thin chicken.

"You'll stay and have dinner, it's the least I can do. I don't know what I was thinking trying to carry so much in one trip." She pulled his tie in her direction leading him into the yard.

Dimitri placed the parcels on the floor just inside the door and was thrust into the yard by the boy. A game of hide and seek was fast afoot. From inside the house Dimitri could hear Fabienne singing as she moved about the small cabin.

"Au clair de la lune, Mon ami Pierrot, Prête-moi ta plume

Pour écrire un mot. Ma chandelle est morte, Je n'ai plus de feu. Ouvre-moi ta porte Pour l'amour de Dieu."

Her voice lifted the soul, stirring, pure and angelic. Dimitri felt a need to be close to her. He followed the boy into the main room of the cottage. Fabienne had already made a fire and was preparing a meal, chopping vegetables and herbs and placing them into a pot. Dimitri was eager to help. She took his hand and sat him down, kissing him on the forehead. She smiled and pushed a pipe across the table, closer to his chair.

"You sit."

"I should help entertain young Henri?"

"He will be at my aunt's tonight."

Dimitri was intrigued by the way this alluring conversation was taking shape. The prospect of enjoying a home-cooked meal and the quiet company of this beautiful woman, was serendipitous and indeed, delightfully unexpected.

The small room filled with warmth. Fabienne took a break from the cooking and sat down next to Dimitri.

She playfully took the pipe from his lips and took a lengthy drag from it. She let the warm smoke flow effortlessly from her mouth. Smiling, she returned to the kitchen, stroked the fire and filled two small cups with a welcome pinot noir.

"How do you not have to be with your other soldiers? Won't you find your way into trouble with your commanders?" she wondered.

"I move papers and information, usually as fast as possible, it's my job. I work alone mostly, and had a few days of R&R due me, I have to keep moving, and I'm not expected back by my superiors till early next week," he told her.

"Now, I have just the thing to slow your work plans to a more forgiving schedule. I'm filling that bathtub with the hottest water I can stand and I'm going to clean every trace of mud from my body, from that awful road."

Fabienne placed herself on Dimitri's lap holding the cups of wine in her hands.

"You look a little muddy, too," she added.

Dimitri allowed himself a smile, as Fabienne gently gave him a tiny kiss on the lips. He watched the cadence of her body intently as she walked back into the kitchen. He promised the desire that electrified his skin that he would indeed work slowly.

The pair sat and talked well after dinner, his hand resting on hers. The last aromatic spoonful of her stew was something special, something to cherish. He licked the back of the spoon clean.

"Have you always been a singer?' he asked.

"What? Me? Well no, it's just a nice way to say goodnight to my little one," she said.

"I enjoyed hearing you and I think you should do it more often, perhaps as part of a church choir."

"You're generous, that is very kind of you. I have been without church for a long time."

"A large community may be helpful for the boy, now and especially in his later years," he said.

"I think that makes sense. It's the intimate part of the congregation that I'm having an issue with, people who are however well-meaning keep attempting to marry me off. To hell with them, I'm here to make my own choices," she declared.

Dimitri waited before he responded. The flicker of candlelight was a graceful complement that kept his gaze fixed on the richness of her eyes. She was illuminated, framed in warmth, with an edge of light that barely reached her face resting romantically on one cheek, falling darker into the shadow of her almost unseen shoulders. He was mesmerized.

She spoke at a level just higher than a whisper and he moved closer than would be otherwise acceptable. "I grew up on this little farm, I love it here, but now so much has changed," she said.

"If you could change one thing, one piece, what would it be?" he asked.

"That's a hard one to answer, and it would take some daring, but I often thought of living in Brittany, near the coast. I've never been, it could be a new adventure."

A slight gust of wind encircled them. He could feel her breath as she spoke. When he replied to her their lips were inches apart and moving closer. A deep kiss followed, affirming a feeling that had enjoined them from the moment they met.

Fabienne excused herself to start filling the pot with water for the bath, her hand running through her hair as she turned. It would take some time to raise the water to a boil and a number of pots were needed to fill the tub. His anticipation grew as he offered to help with the well water, but Fabienne told him to relax.

He wondered if the oversized wooden tub had been a piece of harvesting equipment at one point. It was a coarse barrel, wood and metal, clearly repurposed, and perfectly suited for bathing. Fabienne gathered water in two large cauldrons which she hung over the flames, and each time she passed the chair a new piece of clothing was removed and placed loosely on the seat. She used her time in a resourceful manner. Waiting for the water to boil, she worked on opening the buckles and leather straps that covered Dimitri's uniform, careful to keep his side arm and bullets away on a high shelf. Fabienne removed his shirt buttons one-by-one, taking time to enjoy his approving smile as she moved down his body. Pulling the shirt above his belt, she paused to hold him around his waist. His muscles were taut and firm. Dimitri was precise with his uniform folding it and taking care not to get it wet. He stepped towards her, expecting her to retreat. She moved closer allowing their bodies to touch.

She pointed to the tub, directing him to take his seat. Fabienne poured the bucket of water near his toes. First one, then the next.

"That's hot!"

"I know, keep it warm for me," she said with a coy smile.

She turned to refill the pots. Dimitri wet a cloth and began to rub his body, starting with his neck. Fabienne returned, placing the pots above the fire. She stood backlit by the flames, letting her dress fall to the floor. Dimitri studied every inch of her body. She touched his arm as she lifted her leg over the side of the tub, coming to rest seated across from him.

"This is wonderful, we need more water!"

"I'm working slowly," he replied.

As she sat in the water, Dimitri squeezed her legs entwining hers with his, and the two of them laughed as she playfully splashed his chest.

As she poured the next pot over his head, he focused on her wet fire-lit body, as she moved from the edge of the tub back toward the fire. Each drop of water clung tightly to her skin, sparkled and then ran down the length of her legs to the growing puddle on the floor. He reached for her as she stepped back into the water. His hands held her tightly around the curve of her illuminated waist as he lowered her body into the tub.

"I've been alone for a long...," she confessed quietly.

"We'll do this together," interjecting her in a calm and reassuring voice.

Dimitri sat up and began to softly kiss her below the navel; steadily working his way lower, slowly, but with exuberance. The tickle of his breath on her toned skin made her flinch and gasp, the perfect pre-kiss tease. He moved lower igniting a sensual quintessence. She held the top of his head in her hands, pressing him firmly into her, pulling his hair. Covered in water, he continued with purpose, succulently exploring with his tongue and lips. Apprehension and consuming self-awareness faded. An intimate offering accompanied her newly found inhibition, allowing her to relax as she sat lower and deeper into her hips.

Dimitri savored her warmth in between his rhythmic movements and unrehearsed long strokes artfully leading, and reacting to a racing heart's tempo. All of his senses were piqued and surrounded by her, he felt both peaceful and determined. He held her with his hands and mouth, cradling her as if these were the fleeting minutes of his last day on earth. She felt energized with each touch. For a moment she almost controlled the escalating sharp movements coming from her hips, her breathing grew heavy and deep, her legs tightened. Her hands firmly cupped her breasts as her body shook. Her feet splashed the water when she exhaled in a low moan. Dimitri supported her weight as she lost her balance, trying to catch her breath.

Dimitri laid her down, she was motionless and calm in the water. He poured two more cauldrons of hot water into the bath that made Fabienne hum approvingly. Steam and moisture hovered above her skin. In the wet darkness the chatter of her own thoughts dissipated, granting her a blissful short-lived moment of solitude. He tugged gently on her long wet hair that curved down her back urging her back to his side of the tub. He held her tightly. She kissed his cheek and moved her knees apart to lie on top of him. Slowly at first, she rocked her body over his firm stomach. She smiled and then kissed his neck and reached her arms out and down to hold his muscular body. Urgently she slid her body down raising her hips to mount tightly around him.

"Oui! Maintenant," she whispered.

They moved together and apart finding unison, a physical and emotional display of compatibility rarely seen. The depth of his passion was intense, a lust-fueled tension touching anger, which grew as she rode on top of him. She looked deeply into his eyes, her mouth hung open, she uttered unfinished words that grew louder and louder. Dimitri lifted himself to his feet, holding her ass in both hands, her arms draped around his neck. Her breasts pressed into his body as she was hoisted up and down. With a raging vigor, his unconquered cadence blissfully continued, and continued. The energy building between them heightened and was almost unbearable, her liberating surrender followed.

"Oui!" she screamed.

She could take no more, the power and speed of his movements were animal in nature.

"Oui!"

Her body was covered in moisture; water, steam, and sweat. Her fingers dug into his back, as she started shaking uncontrollably. With mutual purpose and forcefulness, they clung to one another, as he failed to fend off the explosive tension flowing out of his body.

He held her close as Fabienne slowly wrapped her legs around him, holding him tightly. As they stood as one in the darkness, they kissed and laughed at the amount of water that surrounded them on the floor.

The pair playfully sparred over a small towel in a valiant attempt to dry themselves standing by the fire. Through the lattice of the paned glass window over her shoulder, he noticed the moonlit sparkle from a thin layer of ice forming on the tree branches outside. On any other night he would have dismissed or forgotten to stop to experience the glorious visual symphony beginning to take place in the darkness. The soothing enjoyment and simplicity of the reflection, sparkling in the small frozen droplets, brought a quiet calm to his soul as the branches swayed. In stillness, he felt grateful for this new connection and clung to her with an appreciation for the humanity that allowed this affaire de coeur. At long last, he discovered the foundation, the building blocks of what it means to feel at home. Between them was a mysteriously powerful bond, a refreshing sense of belonging that was meaningful, yet under expressed. They reached a level of trust, which had always been elusive for him. He couldn't permit what they shared to be lost in idle sinful desire or a strident void of primal lust. There was a rising sincerity in the powerful grip that pulled him toward her allowing them to share tingling moments of self-depre-cating humor that counterbalanced the seriousness of their passionate decisions.

Dimitri summoned his last bit of energy, turning toward a bed held in a wooden frame at the far end of the cottage. Under the heavy blanket he watched Fabienne work a brush through her raven-colored hair and cover herself in a night-gown with a small cap protecting her braid. As she attempted to lay down, Dimitri playfully reached towards her and was pushed away. Again, he pulled her near and she rebuffed him; his third effort was more substantial and committed. He lifted her and moved her close, right next to him.

"Okay," she laughed, acknowledging how futile it was to fight the embrace that came next. He held her tightly, as he reflected on what had just happened. Between yawns, he hoped for sleep or at least to feel a part of the peace and stillness that would lead to the hopeful beginning of a blissful dream.

The rain falling on the roof woke him gently and made him smile and he was thinking perhaps if it lasted or got heavy it would delay his departure. The sound of water held professional value, it was an effective method of protection masking his movements while on duty. Working in the rain, he had an advantage to those who wouldn't dare. The sound of rain allowed him to move undetected, the falling raindrops insulated him, giving him cover. Standing by a river or stream, he could sing to himself and it would go unnoticed. Away from the road or near the forest, a dry leaf would announce his presence and bring significant problems to a stealth courier. It was different for farmers and soldiers then it was for regular people. An individual outside during weather for an extended time, a project was likely underway. A merchant could sometimes delay, but Dimitri and his brothers had no choice. He fell back asleep and woke before Fabienne. He quietly got out of bed and dressed himself next to the large tub. He smiled at the fact that there was still water on the floor from earlier that night. His amusement faded when he looked toward the door. The door was change, the directed gamble of a one-way exit, ushering in more of the unknown, more uncertainty. It could be a promised-filled gateway, or a terror laden path to KDD. He returned to Fabienne.

"I have to get moving."

"But the rain?" she worried.

"It's fine, it's gentle, and will serve me well. I will find you on my way home, my return, I mean," he stumbled, "I should be no longer than a week."

"Au revoir mon amour." She whispered.

"For Henri," he placed his whistle on the bedside table.

He kissed her, and somehow pulled himself from her lingering embrace. Her perfume infiltrated his uniform. He opened the door with his campaign hat firmly in place, ready to face the weather. It was early, and the rain and mud would dampen the sounds of his boots. Two hours would pass before the soft texture of her embroidered handkerchief tucked in his jacket pocket would get his attention. The morsels of hard bread and the sweet, tart taste of black currant marmalade drew a smile to his lips as he licked them clean, and imagined his swift return.

WALK AWAY

THEY WERE SILENT on the walk away with hearing damaged, their skulls racked with endless ringing. Exiting the turmoil was an order from command with a burst of hope. The saintly notion of survival was foundational, but the urgent wish for dry feet and cleaner boots was the ultimate desire. The wounded on both sides shared a common desperate wish to be removed to an established aid center. Shouted triage questions greeted them at the rear lift of a small truck that served as the first step toward a transport carriage. They were still just a few minutes walk from the front, the journey further granted three days away, not for R&R, they were still on duty. This interlude was just long enough to eat, bathe, dry out socks, and tend to rotten wet feet. It was a break after two weeks in combat to find a glimpse of a sane thought and worry again with the vexing mental stress of knowing the return to a wet trench was fast approaching. Being stationed in the tent was never long enough to heal or feel anything other than the growing pressure of knowing that the opportunity to race towards one's own demise was looming in the near future. KDD, KDD haunted the repeating echo of ringing lingering in their eardrums. No one slept or said more than three words, but each was grateful for a hot meal, fresh socks, and a dry cot. A visit to the barbershop tent was the capstone to the remaking process.

One didn't encounter friendliness in a combat-zone – alliances born out of concern and survival became ironclad in earnest. Dimitri met Sam, the barber, when they trained together in England, a joyful distant memory diametrically opposed to their current situation. The barbershop was a familiar setting for enlisted and officers alike. Sam's comfortable setting afforded an unvarnished opinion to be freely amplified and discussed among ridicule, speculation, and assorted empirical laws. Weighty positions of philosophy, shy politics were lightly spread and reexamined, accepted, or curtly challenged. Sam usually had a stinging retort. Located in his barracks - the barbershop was the ultimate sanctuary. Officers had their own day that felt a bit more formal. All the men sought relaxed conversation and a space void of a mission where they could be carefree for a short while. It was a time for spirited camaraderie. Some found peace and felt protected by Sam's prayers. Being together, free from being volunteered, is something all the men sought. Without knowing it, being at Sam's made the passing moments feel soulful and intimate.

Stories of accomplishment and espionage were commonly embellished and overly presented. Successful campaigns and heroic exploits taunted Sam who was assigned to a tent working a scissor and a broom. Dimitri had the honor of cutting Sam's hair, an interesting twist of brotherhood and trust. In these private moments Sam would cry to him about his predicament and his desire to be reassigned to a combat role. Sam would apologize for what he felt was hubris as Dimitri would urge him to stay put.

"I'm just so bored cutting hair." Sam complained.

"You're alive, Shane bought it yesterday, stay here," he pleaded.

"I just need to do more. I would switch with you in a heartbeat, no pun intended." Sam continued.

"You can't see past the points of a scissor. That is a good thing, you have a trade."

Dimitri's words landed firmly with Sam. Their kinship grew as they passed through England, and became cemented following a dust-up with a Captain where Dimitri interceded in the heated exchange with a superior officer. Risking rank and a jail cell, Dimitri challenged the out-of-turn Captain squarely toe-to-toe. The confrontation granted Sam a successful outcome, not an apology, but rather "Never mind," as if the lambasting hadn't taken place. Sam was shaken, awash in fear, and took solace in Dimitri's devilish smile. Their loyalty was heightened by the intensity of the Captain's misplaced projection towards Sam. Dimitri swiftly flagged the Captain's friendly fire missive sensing his leadership shortcomings, and the needless verbal attack on his friend. Quietly, he was relieved, and Dimitri was aglow wiping the sweat from his forehead. Having the unique ability to speak truth to power was an elusive skillset, but to stand up to command, when it mattered, was saintly.

The months that followed established routine. Sam found the safe, predictable events to be insufferable, yet ironically, his dry boots and warm barracks were envied by every customer who sat in his chair. Searching through the heart of his current existence, his deep Jewish faith and practice, Sam was unable to reconcile his current assignment and his larger overmastering desire to participate. His mind was calm and still as he lit his second cigar. Sam's eyes looked directly at the rack of uniforms beyond the chair; each would allow him to find a ride to the front. Sam swirled the smoke taking his cigar from his lip and started to work his broom.

In the weeks that followed, Dimitri was a frequent visitor to Sam's tent.

"You're too clean for combat," Sam announced, welcoming him back.

"Me? Really?" Dimitri returned.

"You're in here every three days," Sam teased. "I guess Fabienne the seamstress has a weakness for clean shaven reasonably charming, holy unreliable, junior grade officers or some configuration of the same."

"Distinction without a difference." Dimitri explained.

"Such a shame, a whole career of failing upwards." Sam pressed harder.

"Keep going." Dimitri playfully encouraged.

"Hell, you'll probably run this mess before long. She's in back," Sam continued.

"I'm just trying to keep the most important things in the world close to me." Dimitri explained.

"Smart."

"Everything you do is an excuse for failure, an apology for being a man!" Dimitri announced.

"Ouch, is that the best you can do? Thanks for listening, lock up when you leave." Sam had the last word and relished the spirited nature of his time with Dimitri.

"Stop that," Fabienne demanded as Dimitri entered the connecting tent, "these words can hurt. Sam has been a godsend, to both of us."

"I know and he knows how I feel, that's how we tease each other." Dimitri's embarrassed explanation revealed a sincere wish to be forgiven, but more so, expressed clearly to both of them, that her opinion of him mattered.

"Just take a bit of caution, he has a heavy amount of politics around him and he adds his own pressure seeing all of you return from the front. Sometimes he feels like he's not a part of the effort," she continued. Her work finishing uniforms could be interrupted long enough for the war to pause for both of them for a much needed and overdue visit.

"Okay, I will," he assured her taking her hand.

"I don't have all day, I have to get back to these shirts, but I appreciate you came to find me, are you hungry?" She moved closer ignoring his whispered answer. Her embrace would need to make sure her lips or tears didn't mark his dress uniform.

"We should, if it makes sense. When it's all over we can find that spot by the coast. You can tailor, Sam has a trade, and I can work on a boat, what do you say? You remember the coast?" He asked.

"Of course, I love the idea, take care of Sam too please."

Leaving the tent, Dimitri promised to stay focused on Sam and Fabienne both of whom had become important and cherished parts of his life. Dimitri's dispatches would keep on the move for another day or two at most.

• • •

Powerful feelings of guilt for being jealous of his fellow soldiers kept Sam awake in bed. His greatest vulnerability was his lust and desire to achieve valor and victory, but sincerity drove him to want to participate in a more meaningful way.

Two days later, Sam loaded his rifle and wearing a uniform that wasn't his, made his way to the forward trench. KDD was vacant, void of life, completely isolated. The full attention of so many at the same time was hyper-focused on killing and death. Would anything survive? Even a faint memory of what it takes to support existence, replant an ecosystem reassured of growth and renewal was elusive, and overmatched by bloodlust. Fear and unnatural terror was expelled in the unrelenting flash of explosions shadowed by rolling smoke. Dimitri didn't have the time to fully unpack how furious he was to see Sam's arrival.

"You sure? This is coming fast!" Dimitri shouted.

Letters to loved ones left out moments prior to an advance. While rechecking weapons, many said a quiet prayer and took a final glance at a locket or photograph.

"Two minutes."

"Get quick, if you get hit, stay down. I will come for you. I'm not letting you do this alone. Your sidearm loaded? Mask up."

Surrounded by the exploding shells, Sam longed for his familiar chair, where his ear heard everything, and he would be back in the know.

HOLD TIGHT

SAM WAS QUICK and still running as the first bullet tore through his chest, and his eyes were locked wide open as his body absorbed the contorting force and trauma. His last image on earth was of a stream of blood flowing from his nose and his startled mouth. A second round shot through his right leg driving him hard into the dirt. Reaching for him, Dimitri tripped on a row of barbed wire, landing squarely on top of Sam.

"I think I smudged the uniform," Sam confessed in his last breath.

With quick action Dimitri used his belt to tourniquet his leg and put pressure on his chest. Sam's collapsed body shielded Dimitri and was shot twice more.

"Medic! Medic!"

Silence was the only response. To his right a charge of bayonets raced toward each other. Heavy footsteps were followed by the agonizing sounds of fading life and the pulling embrace of death. Plunging blades sliced deeply into butchered bodies of the doomed enemy. Exploding eyeballs and a projected cough of blood demonstrated that the length of one's arms mattered with bayonets. Directly in front of their position, a group of men were sprinting towards him. Dimitri drew his sidearm and took dead aim at the figures moving in the toxic smog.

"HOLD! Hold tight soldier," a voice ordered, "We'll help you."

The men had made it into the German trench, cleared a machine gun and killed eight of the enemy. Four of the men lifted Sam, advancing his lifeless body to the German line.

It wasn't essential where command found him, in the book of life what he sacrificed and how he paid was significant. He was gone, dead, but later that day others would be alive because of his selfless effort. Sam's bravery and the successful advance would brand his battlefield death as heroic. Dimitri understood the weight of a well-earned medal. His colleagues could measure a soldier more completely looking at an adorned uniform. Sam's parents' concern would become Dimitri's next priority-find the Rabbi and ensure a proper and timely burial. It was important to Dimitri to make sure everything was handled urgently and with the full measure of Sam's faith, he owed it to him and would make sure of it, just so he could let his family know. Shocked and stunned faces greeted the arrival of Sam's body at the aid station.

"He literally told me yesterday he'd outrun them all, why Sam? Why?" The driver implored.

"He just wanted to do his part," Dimitri offered, "he definitely saved my skin. I need to get him moved fast."

"No problem, next transport. I'll take care of him, glad you're on your feet," the driver assured him.

Dimitri responded by tossing a small pouch of tobacco to the driver.

Saying goodbye was a struggle. His itchy heart scratched his throat when he breathed. He clung to Sam's body for a moment that wasn't long enough and through the flow of tears offered the send off from command at Salisbury.

"Wishing you godspeed and hope you stay safe as you continue your onward journey."

Dimitri offered a salute, wiped Sam's brow, turned and was off.

The next step required some doing. Before reaching the Rabbi, Dimitri climbed through the window of Sam's quarters adjacent to the barbershop. In the bottom of Sam's chest was a smooth satchel that held Sam's tallit and a volume of Hebrew prayers.

The paper that fell from the prayer book was unexpected and was addressed to Dimitri.

Hey Pal,
If you're reading this, my plan didn't go so well – forgive me. You gave me sound advice and I played my hand and tried to do my part. Don't let it ruin your weekend. I sent my folks a bunch of my pay, but here's some tips I left for you. Just wanted to say thanks and I appreciate everything you did for me. Give my chair to the next lucky guy, give him a cigar and my broom, hopefully he'll have something to say and will stay put. Or better still, grab the scissors yourself – good advice. Stay healthy.

Love,
Sam

Rabbi Mendi did what he could to distract and console Dimitri from his grief, but they had a burial to focus on and having that task before them was helpful. The Rabbi briefly explained the Tachrichim a burial shroud that covered Sam's body. A pine casket would be secured as his body was moved to the cemetery for Jewish-American Soldiers. The Rabbi's prayers filled the tent as Sam's body was placed in the coffin. Dimitri was directed to cut the long corner tzitzit removing it from the tallit. The prayers continued. Dimitri silently thanked Sam for his friendship, his sacrifice, and for keeping him alive. He committed to making sure Sam's family would receive his belongings, the piece of his tallit and a letter from command noting his contribution to the war effort. And lastly, Rabbi Mendi would send word describing how Sam kept true to his faith and shared a dedication to his fellow soldiers. A small passage would assure the family that Sam's resting place and burial was Rabbinical and appropriate in all aspects.

HALF MOON

THE PROSPECT OF heading home felt magical. They knew orders would follow soon and a journey would begin. The early morning that followed a sleepless night was relaxing, a peaceful expression of celebration and joy. Dimitri was eternally restless. His high level of exhaustion was counterbalanced by exuberance that tingled his body. He spent the lion's share of the night motionless studying every detail of the half moon beyond his window. He was out early, no one wanted to miss or be late to get more news about the end of the war.

Dimitri's wish was to find Fabienne and make the trek to Brittany, but he knew that would have to wait. Happily, he would still have to follow routine, staying regimented would help keep a needed sense of order amid a vast transition. He took sanctuary in the warmth of these moments and memories they shared together.

Eli had his own sense of timing, which often left Dimitri sitting alone at the table staring toward the street. The one remaining wall of the café was an important constant for the pair. The table was set in a shadowed rear corner, as bright light shined through the main door that held no glass. The room was in shambles. Veronique stood in the middle of the remnants of her establishment pensively weighing her future options. Quietly, she drew on a cigarette, and was thankful that her neighboring house was untouched. She imagined rebuilding, but knew that might not be realistic. The ceiling above was open to the sky, the remains of a once grand chandelier hung from a fractured timber high above her. She managed to serve hot tea and keep an assortment of cheese for her few, yet loyal, clients. Dimitri focused on the chipped and broken tiles on the table and in the frames that surrounded him. He gazed intently, hoping to piece together in his mind the painted fragments, knowing they would reveal a complete and loving storyboard. A blue teacup in front of him was trimmed in gold, a mixed unmatched cup looking for a saucer. The place setting across from him was a bright sunburst yellow trimmed in black, a unique and elegant collection. Remarkably they were not cracked or chipped. The buttery smell of croissants baking filled the restaurant with a lush and welcoming aroma.

Dimitri heard a motorcycle and knew Eli was soon approaching. Veronique checked her hair, wiped her forehead and started to move briskly about the modest kitchen. Eli parked across the street and hopped on to the sidewalk. His gait was buoyant.

"Where is my girl? Veronique? Mademoiselle?" he called as he strolled in.

"Sit please, I'm here," she called, from behind the wall. Eli was excited by her voice. He first noticed her flowing floral dress from his motorcycle months ago, as she was walking to start breakfast that morning. He had to be near her and he'd been by her side every day since.

She arrived with tea and a plate of cheese with two small croissants. Eli stood and embraced her, taking a few extra moments to let the events of the last twenty-four hours sink in.

"They've done it, right? No one backed out? What now?" Dimitri wondered. His oversized grin greeted his friend.

"We all have another day to enjoy." Veronique added reaching her arms to touch Eli and Dimitri. The three moved toward each other in solidarity thankful for the end of conflict. Her eyes began to tear and she laughed as she sighed in relief. How were they able to survive? What fortune? What luck? Her reflections became a blessing which offered personal insight and perspective; she would never allow her valuable time to be idle or consumed with doubt.

"Come sit with me, darling" Eli urged, reaching towards her.

"No, no, a girl has to eat, I have much too much to do."

"I will find you tonight, after we hear what's next for us," he laughed.

Eli's joke wasn't lost on Dimitri, the landscape had shifted and the two would have to reconfigure their approach to work and try to look out for each other as the unit and their responsibilities wound down. The goal of movement and keeping near command became a priority.

"What's the timeline on this? We're not moving out right away, are we?" Dimitri asked.

"I saw the Major yesterday," Eli explained, "it felt like we are doing business as usual. Based on what I can tell, two months?"

Eli looked around the café to see if Veronique was in earshot.

"I don't know if two months is going to apply to everyone," Eli whispered, "they may slim the crew down or keep some of us nearby for a longer time frame."

Dimitri almost confided in Eli his wish to find Fabienne. He could see the street coming to life over Eli's shoulder. One cup of tea followed another. The topic of change brought worry and an obvious layer of tension to Dimitri's body reaching his forehead. Eli was eager to find the opportunity in this new operational climate. He loved a new challenge and was excited by change. Dimitri asked Eli about Brittany. Eli had traveled across the channel months earlier and stopped in Saint-Malo, a walled city with a rich history.

"You can't stand to leave, it's just about as close to a fantasy as you can find. It's a city surrounded by sea, with a cathedral overhead, entirely breathtaking, and it dates back to forever ago," Eli explained.

It could be perfect for him and Fabienne to escape to after his service. He was thrilled to hear of the historic location. He smiled and thought maybe he'd have the courage to ask the Major for the time to visit. He eased back in the chair thinking about a new opportunity, as he stretched his body, finishing a smoke with Eli. The restful calm wouldn't last beyond a single cigarette.

The crash of the first potato masher that rained down on the square was a sound the men had both heard before. The handle landed first. Their eyes widened as their adrenaline propelled them instantly to attention. The first explosion pushed their bodies low as they ducked for cover. The deafening blast was followed by haunting silence. Alone in the street a small child let out a piercing scream. She was crying, standing by her mother, who was unconscious and bleeding on the ground. Fearless and fast, they sprung into action.

"Come on," Eli shouted.

Dashing off the curb Eli reached for the little girl, and as he did a single bullet fired from an upper window pierced his body below his chin. Veronique screamed from inside the café as Eli fell back onto the ground. Across the road two men returned fire toward the window above giving

Dimitri the cover needed to almost reach the dying woman and her little girl. He reached for his gun, pulling his side arm from its holster as he exited the doorway. He heard the sound of another stielhandgranate landing behind him. He leaped as the stick grenade explosion erupted lifting him higher and throwing him further into the air. The impact of landing on his head left him listless and still. A pool of blood from the tear of his fractured skull stained the road, flowing between the curves of the smooth round rocks. The shrill sounds of screaming, KDD, continued.

Veronique's body leaned heavily against the doorframe. She could see Eli gasping with a breath that would fade and soon be gone. Her legs were weak; her hand covered her mouth as she watched the horror play out in front of her. She couldn't feel the tears that had funneled to her lips. Slowly, she stepped into the street walking toward him, unable to hear the shouting and shooting that continued. She knelt when she reached his body, his uniform drenched in blood. She kissed his face and hugged him tightly.

An intense pain gripped her chest making breathing a struggle. She could only cough and scream to fight the growing anguish. She kissed him again and knew it was goodbye.

"Come, my child," she said extending her hand out to the little girl next to her. Standing, the toe of her black leather shoe pierced the edge of the glossy puddle flowing from Eli's body. She ushered the child in the direction of the restaurant leaving behind a partial solitary footprint.

The killing would come to an abrupt end after the attacker was finally shot and urgently tossed into the street to signal to the neighborhood exactly who was responsible. The official report would later say anarchists with the goal of continuing the conflict were to blame for the carnage.

Three farmers lifted Dimitri moving him onto a wagon. There was only one place he could get the needed care, and time was of the essence. He was still and covered in blood. Looking out through the blood-splattered doorframe, Veronique could see Father Louis running toward the woman's body, with a bible in his hand. She held tightly to the little girl, whose name she didn't yet know. In the supportive embrace, Veronique promised herself that she would protect this child, always.

SAINT CLAIRE

I T WAS TWO weeks before he could stand and find his way to supporting his full weight. Walking would be next, following intense exercise and a routine to strengthen his body and develop muscle memory. Nurse Claire was happy to see his commitment to physical culture benefit his progress, but she had been here before and knew it was too soon to call this stage a recovery.

"Excellent work today, little one," Claire teased. "Try to get some rest. You and I have a busy day of exercise in the morning."

Claire spoke to Dimitri as though he were just a little boy, innocent and in need of coddling. Her protective nature made perfect sense after the amount of death and injuries she endured during the war. She had a honed maternal instinct. Her goal for herself, and others was simple – survival, to reset and return to good-natured optimism with abundant humor, complementing a joyous demeanor.

Claire paused to reflect on the progress of her last patient. She had made herself a promise; she was done with the blood, death, and war. Done with it, all of it, she could suffer no more. The emotional strain had taken a toll on her and in quiet moments she would smoke, drink, and curse the fates that permitted her to experience the depth of tragedy she lived through. The hardened stare from her dark eyes expressed the extent of the repeated loss of life and trauma that she endured. Turning the injured away would be the only solution, an option she couldn't bring herself to consider.

She remembered the nurse's station was dismantled in time to transport the wounded. A grateful Command ensured a reinforcement of supplies and inventory which allowed her to redeploy to the farmhouse, its rehabilitation and function as a field hospital were the result. When Dimitri arrived, he was ushered into the main room, unconscious and covered in blood. He was positioned on her large wooden table that divided the large space.

"Here? Now? Bring him to your parlor!" She bellowed.

Her last dress free of bloodstains was now another sacrifice to the service of the wounded. She had promised and was expected at the concert to celebrate the newest version of found peace. She imagined sweeping arpeggio runs of the piano, uplifted by strings and song, and a night away from the abyss of never-ending insomnia and the death dreams of war.

"Ines! Water at once, bring me bandages, my kit!" she commanded in a voice that was elevated.

Her urgent directives were followed to the letter. Her partner rapidly moved around the number of rooms, in and out of drawers, to bring the nurse her supplies and elixirs. The farmers were well acquainted with Nurse Claire's domineering personality and moved away slowly. The fact remained she was highly regarded, having served the role of neighborhood hospital and doctor for most of her life. Dimitri lay spread eagle on the table, a slick of blood grew to the edge of the table, falling in thin lines to the floor.

Nurse Claire opened a leather case full of medical instruments, while Ines removed Dimitri's clothes. She found four minor shrapnel wounds, and then the main wound to his head. She noticed a large swollen area near his right shoulder, but was relieved to see his collarbone was still intact. She washed his head with a mixture of anesthetic and took notice of the small fracture of his skull. A gentle application of chloroform was applied near his nose to keep him motionless. She would attempt to close the wound and bandage him, but she was concerned of possible swelling of the meninges and pressure on his brain. Suturing the four shrapnel wounds followed, and she took care to make sure that the metal was removed and no clothing had entered his wounds.

"Ines, help me wash him and let's get a night shirt for him from the armoire," she asked.

Nurse Claire was happy to see movement in his chest his faint breath gave her hope. She smiled contently, relieved, and knowing with certainty this had to be her very last patient of the war. The two women worked on opposite sides of him to wash the blood from his skin. He would stay in place for the time being; the next morning she would gather a group to help carry him by stretcher to a waiting bed.

Ines was tired of the blood, the smell of death, and seeing another man dying. She kept to her work and allowed herself a smile, realizing the irony that in spite of their skills and collective effort, many of the men that Claire encounters - died. Would this be different? Ines didn't say much, but she heard it all, and possessed a natural ability to sense what was left unmentioned inside every conversation. The pair survived together, covered in blood and surrounded by never ending death for more than a year. They were a life force for a multitude of soldiers and became a support structure for each other, affection and a loving relationship followed. Having each other nurtured a bond, creating a sanctuary from war and the horror of constant death.

In spite of her youth, Ines was currently exhausted by men and the things men do. She had lived too much of the sour dreams and empty promises, while suffering repeatedly at the abusive hands of those who came calling. Claire changed this construct. In safety and success they connected harmoniously, flourishing alongside the chaos and ruin around them.

The following morning the house was quiet. Claire had arranged with the help of the milk driver and the farmer across the field to move Dimitri to a spare room reserved as a recovery space. No thanks was needed, the men were happy to be in her good graces, Dimitri was unconscious for two days. In his first movement he slowly reached for the bandage that covered his eyes.

"Can you hear me?" Claire asked.

"Where am I?" Dimitri replied with a growl.

"Keep the bandage on for now, please. You are with me, I am Nurse Claire, you need to rest. You'll be on your feet soon."

"What happened?" Dimitri asked, "my head is pounding."

"Rest, please, please, there will be plenty of time to catch you up." The questioning and the personal assessment was encouraging to Claire.

" I need to find the toilet, is there an outhouse?"

"Use this bedpan. I will help you," Nurse Claire moved closer.

He wasn't shy and he urgently needed to go. Claire had little use for men, and in the humanity of the recovery process that she experienced every day she was seldom surprised.

"Alright, now take a sip of this water, and swallow a spoonful of this it will help you rest," she urged.

He was completely still, out for the thirty-six hours that followed. The smell of food cooking filled the air welcoming him in from the darkness, "Hello?" Dimitri called.

"Ines, check the boy." Claire directed.

"Slowly now." Ines said entering the bedroom.

"Where, Where am I? Can I take this off?" he asked pulling at his bandage.

"Let me do it, I need to give you a clean one and will let you see," Ines promised.

"Who are you?" Dimitri asked.

"You are here with Nurse Claire, I'm Ines, how do you feel?"

"Tired, so tired, what happened? This headache," He touched his forehead.

"The anarchists tried to keep fighting in the square." Ines told him.

"What fight? And there was a girl? Wait, I have a buddy named, named Eli?" He drew a blank, confusion followed, and deep fear gripped him.

"Nurse Claire, he's ready for you, please," Ines called.

"Eli? Right, Eli!" Dimitri tried to reassure himself that the reality he couldn't remember was untrue.

"Steady. I'm so sorry, my dear, Eli's gone." Claire said softly entering the room. She was ironically relieved to have a responsive patient who could converse and reply, despite learning the somber news.

The words were perplexing to Dimitri. His breath stopped as he struggled to remember what happened. He stared at Ines, who moved away slowly.

"I know it's not your fault," Dimitri said reaching for her.

He tried to stand and stumbled on to the bed, as his knee fell heavily to the floor. His fist punched the bed.

"Eli, oh Eli," he moaned, pushing his forehead into the pillow.

"I'm sorry precious one," Nurse Claire touched his shoulder in an attempt to console him, "he's gone. Eli was honored for his bravery and attempting to save the child."

"Eli," Dimitri repeated.

"Your men were present and turned out in numbers and so did this community. There were a number of medals and recognitions, one is near the clean uniform and boots your unit delivered. You are conscripted to my care. Father Louis has asked those who walk in faith to support Veronique and the child she adopted. The generosity of your men was appropriately noted."

"Right, that's right, Veronique and the little girl. So, she and...," he paused attempting to almost remember what Veronique almost looked like, "they're alive?" Dimitri asked.

"Yes."

"Thank goodness."

Dimitri wiped his tears attempting to recall the conflict. Nurse Claire gently rubbed his back.

Every cherished memory, or at least any important memory worth remembering, was an experience he had shared with Eli. They were gone, his life, he could almost remember, it was faint enough to make him weak and nauseous with grief.

"Well the good news for you is that you are healing well, but the challenge is that you landed on your head. You may have a hard time remembering things and we will see how you progress. I need you to rest and take time to find your strength. You've been through the worst of this, and I'm so sorry about Eli."

His hands and arms failed to shield his eyes away from the bright light as the bandage covering his eyes fell. He was in a small sparse room that adjoined the kitchen, a hand-carved crucifix hung on the wall above the bed. He imagined the sturdy, steady hand that held the wooden cross, whittled by a single blade. Was this a memory? He wondered. Beyond his door, filling the main room, he could see sunlight. The entire south wall of the farmhouse was made of windows that filled the space with warmth. Dimitri closed his eyes and fell back asleep.

His slumber was a time free from pain, but it came with a heavy price; a rushed invitation to a debilitating darkness teetering near insanity. The elixir laced with opium that was near his bed felt like a blessing, but he soon learned its presence was a devil's bargain with a heavy shackle. His migraines followed nightmares filled with hallucinations. His recurring visions of endless black snakes flowing from his pores accompanied his slumber nightly.

"ELI!" he shouted from his nightmare.

"ELI!" he shouted again.

Ines ran into the room finding Dimitri just waking up after the horror of toxic serpents and the hell of a battle-filled dream. It took a few seconds for him to recognize and remember where he was.

"Have some water, you must be starving?" she offered.

"It's the middle of the night, I shouldn't bother you, I'm sorry I woke you."

"Let me bring you something, just in case. You haven't eaten in some time."

It dawned on him that he must have been out for a few

days, but he was certain that he didn't know the days of the week. Ines moved quietly about the kitchen returning with a brioche on a plate with a leg from a roasted chicken, placing a fork and a cup of water on the bedside table.

"This smells wonderful, thank you!"

He grabbed the chicken leg with his hands, he was uncertain if he knew how to handle the fork.

The cottage was surrounded by an ample amount of livestock, the usual form of payment for her medical services. Ines made the surplus animals and eggs the foundation of her trading practices. She was artfully resourceful and could source almost any item given enough time. As she covered Dimitri's legs with a blanket, she thought of Claire's dress that had been ruined when he arrived, Ines would find a new one for her, she knew just what to do.

With a few select and unfurled curtains, Ines kept the house dark and remarkably quiet. She carefully covered the wall of windows, leaving only one small lamp for them to work by in the kitchen. Dimitri prayed for a headache, rather than daggers of pain he felt piercing through his head to his shoulders causing him to scream, cup his ears and fall to his knees. He would roll and reel exploring new heights of discomfort reaching every area of his body. Lying on the bed, Dimitri was concentrating, attempting to remember places from home and old times with Eli. He couldn't relive the main parts of these stories, but the locations were not so far off in his mind. He worried he wouldn't ever get his thoughts back. Incapable of remembering the death of a close combat buddy wasn't exactly liberating, but it had unintended consequences, yet to be revealed. Dealing with the death of two close friends, one old, one new, would remain half-understood to Dimitri. The generous construct acknowledged Eli who he remembered to some degree, though his second friend was absent from his memory and would remain beyond his recollection. When the conflict was mentioned in glances and short conversations, the dialogue seemed slightly familiar; close enough for thoughtful inquiry, but far from specific relief. Dimitri tortured himself with what he thought he knew, what may have happened, and what was long forgotten. A widening unjust chasm between what his memory-loss robbed from him, and what he hoped he could one day remember or remake; a deep uneven abyss defined for the cursed and the damned.

Interestingly, he maintained a deep sense and under-standing of the depth of the pain and fear that defined his current condition. Claire was hopeful the pain would lessen as the days passed and she wrote to a former colleague, a surgeon with whom she trained. He candidly told her, the patient won't remember that he can't remember, his frustration will grow to a physical boiling point where he will lash out at anyone or anything. Not out of anger or disdain, but as a result of exhaustion of endless mental and emotional searching.

Ines noted how frustrated he was feeling and next time he spoke of the loss of Eli, she would point out to him the location of Eli's grave, a distant spot far off through the large wall of windows. She hoped the idea of visiting his resting place would keep his motivation to heal at a heightened level. The dark windows at night drew his curiosity and a stare. Rattled confusion made him certain the surren-dered angels and vaulted souls leapt, taking for granted the shape and strength of the pointed trees. They aimed high straight to the heavens, nothing truer, illuminating a direct and faithful purpose. The bend of the other tree was unique and captivating, a twisted trunk extending in two divergent directions exploding outstretched to find the sun. The enormous bifurcated oak then twisted, pointing back to the center. Spirits flowed though the interwoven pattern, dancing on the edges of the divine infinity loop, encased in moonlight night after night.

As he gained the ability to support himself, Ines would set the goal of visiting the burial site, a twenty-minute walk, much of which was uphill. Dimitri kept moving, and when he finished hiking to pay his respects to Eli, he would walk some more. Occasionally his routine of walking would pause as he tried to remember the destination or faint direction that thinly graced his memory. Walking challenged him to remember. Movement soothed his pain, and every new outing was a point of progress.

He had many lengthy conversations with Eli, most of which were a series of clumsy syllables and short phrases. They could have a heart-to-heart in the blink of an eye and half a glance. His feet sank in the snow.

"You were always the first to go. For what it's worth, thank you. You led the way and probably saved my skin. The girl?! You remember, the little girl with the scream? Veronique's got her, they're okay – she's so distraught though. Looks like with your bike, and the funds the town raised they are going to open up a café just over that ridge. You can definitely hear me. So, tell my folks what we did, or tried to do. I'll check in on Stephen once they let me head back. My memory's getting a little better. I'll get reassigned hopefully. Nurse Claire's had me since the truce. I'm heading to the coast once the snow melts though. Remember that's the place I almost asked you about? Then it's straight home if I think about it right. You remember though? Keep an eye on us, I know you always do! You remember the little girl? I can't remember that much, except I can't forget her – her scream at night. Why sleep? You know that KDD sound that doesn't stop and just gets louder and louder. I hope you don't have to try and make it stop. Hey? Did I tell you about Claire?"

Dimitri stepped slowly back from the plot where a headstone would soon rest. Layers of ice and snow surrounded his cold wet feet. The blizzard-covered markers were barely visible, quietly fading into the distance. Their shape was repeated with snowflake precision. But he struggled to remember which step to take, grappling with a new approach, or whether to start a new direction. He knelt down and used his hand to clear a spot where he imagined Eli was resting. Was he resting?

Dimitri imagined how softly the first touch of long ribbons fell far beyond the knee, resting silently. The twirl and ruffle of flags could be twisted and quiet just like those of an apron. He was on the move though, right?

Eli couldn't sit still. His nomadic soul kept searching, but when it found you it was an expressed commitment. And when it found you, you were embraced in comfort and ease of his presence - his absence left an achy growing void. He wasn't resting; he would have too much to do, driving himself to knowing and doing. Dimitri wasn't worried about the gates. Eli had to be checking on the guys they knew. But, everyone is equal in heaven, right? No rank? Dimitri reminisced in a moment of reflection about the briefing table in the forward room of his barracks where "rank" was an afterthought to the priority of the mission and survival. Some fellas outranked others, not with bars and ribbons, but knowledge, heart, and a multitude of medals earned, but not displayed.

Disoriented and detached, he rubbed the frozen ground and thought once more about his closest friend. His half numb fingers could almost feel the rock he would place as a token of remembrance and affinity. As he stood, he whispered the few words of a prayer he fought to remember and turned to find the tracks in the snow that brought him there. Each hand that reached for another branch along the way brought him one step closer to things that looked more and more what looking familiar looked like. When he felt uncomfortable on the near edge of being frightened, he followed the lofty melody of a songbird that led him in the direction homeward.

EACH STEP

O' SHEA, MALLORY, SULLIVAN: Dimitri could remember their names, Cooke, why, he wondered, why wasn't he able to tell their stories. How could he not place where they were? He repeated the names again, timed with each step hoping on hope to light the spark of even a faint memory. Beyond the hazy blur of a mental picture, he could almost make their intangible faces clear.

Nurse Claire stepped at double time pace toward Dimitri who was farther down the stone walkway, and she placed her hand on his arm.

"You may not remember well looking backwards, try to remember looking forward," she said in a whisper. "You will use up such valuable energy struggling with the past. Start anew, right now. Change the protocols. If you remember what is facing you and embrace it, you'll start to remember all the other important things you're missing. Let the pieces find their right place at the right time. Find something new, listen to the world that's all around you."

"I followed the song of the birds that brought me back home."

"Exactly, see those birds; hear their call, hear their whistle, see their different colors and look closely at the plumes and try to remember the melody of their mating calls."

Claire explained, "A poem is more than a blossom of a flower, it's not what you see, it's how you sense the experience, commit to it and how you share or grow through new feelings. What you see is a kiss or a poem, but there is a powerful underlying melody in the music or in the words, each with an explosive chemistry and emotions that drive or guide you. Why is this significant to you? Stay present and feel, allow yourself to heal. The other exercise for you to try will involve you painting me a picture – no, a masterpiece! From memory, pick a subject and study it closely. Never lose your art – keep exploring. We'll start tonight after supper."

Dimitri took her sage advice to heart. In the days that followed, his new daily routine expanded beyond walking slowly through the gardens tortured by his unremembered personal history. It involved listening and looking at the flight of all the local birds. He enjoyed their erratic and nervous urgency pre-flight. He took longer and longer walks, and started noticing the shapes of the clouds. The warm idea of spring was a soothing notion which kept him in the cool damp garden longer then otherwise recommended for recovery. Moving around the grounds deep in concentration seeking the proper subject to paint was a new and valuable pastime. A faint memory of a woman who he had more than kissed was just out of reach for his healing psyche. How far away was she? Was this a reflection of a kiss or the last retort of a torturous dream?

A few weeks later a letter arrived from Paris. Brown, O'Brien and Buckley took time to tell the story of their journey home. "Did you have a chance to read this?" Ines inquired.

"The names are almost familiar, but I can't remember their story, sorry."

He continued to learn how to work a toothbrush and

struggled to remember the shape or color of food, but was able to recall the aroma of everything that was being prepared. Claire and Ines reinforced routine bathing, as the weeks vanish. Ines helped with trimming his nails, but it was the reflection of a windowpane that brought the question.

"Is that me? Is that what I look like? Have you seen me before?"

Nurse Claire arrived with a scissor and a razor as Dimitri's worrisome questions continued. She reminded him not to focus on the past and only to see what is ahead.

"Healing takes time," she reassured him.

The falling clumps of hair teased Dimitri's shoulders with the touch of a spider, the chill reminding him of the nightmares he endured when he first arrived.

"Now look."

A new view into the windowpane showed a handsome clean-shaven man with time to heal and find serenity. He felt reassured and the small beginnings of being confident, because he remembered a fresh haircut was the part of the usual preparation ahead of an anxious meeting about assignments, or worse, being reassigned.

Dimitri was shy, his posture, demeanor and heart remain committed, unchanged, even when he sees Ines and Claire together or apart. He was mindful to only view them with mutual respect. But he asked himself could he remain equally respectful, when he's unable to acknowledge them in the same regard. Was that even possible or just a conflicted notion or achievement? He wondered how significant elevation, rank and status were measured between the pair and decided to address them as equals.

His artistry was slow to develop at first, but the easel that Ines placed by the window became as Claire had hoped, not just a memory exercise, but rather, a relaxing source of needed entertainment.

Challenge accepted, Dimitri selected his subject and asked Nurse Claire not to look at the painting until it was complete. Two months later he offered it to her. His study was a portrait of Nurse Claire, standing dressed in an army nurse's uniform topped with a small cap in a large outdoor space with walls of sunlight behind her. She wore a cloak that was a deep green satin tied around her neck. Her long flowing black hair reached down below her shoulders touching the embroidered detail in goldenrod stitching. A small chicken was depicted by her feet, with a little goat placed near the right let, facing her. Her hands held the edge of the oversized cloak. Her hair was fully lifted by the wind.

"Might just be our party – just me tonight," Dimitri offered with a coy smile.

"You've earned a new beginning and a grand celebration!"

Drinking and an elevated tone led to unbridled conversation as their hands naturally slipped into one another.

"How can I ever repay or thank you?"

"Nonsense! Don't occupy your thoughts with a ledger. We are clear. Your progress is the best reward for Ines and I."

Both noted his strength and stamina had grown to reveal a solid and remarkably more focused outlook.

It was the second half of a long walk that they had taken many times together that led to a new embrace of goals and purpose. Assumptions were freely redirected and dismissed, where were they? What did the time tell? How did they understand potential in a future context? Candor heightened understanding, finding trust with misplaced desires. The end of the conflict brought closure and presented a new opportunity to feel and pursue widespread life-affirming priorities. Claire had quietly dreamed of motherhood. A notion easily dismissed and delayed given the hostile environment in which they lived. She spent her time wondering if she could allow herself to be taken care of by others.

Two more weeks of silence passed past. Dimitri's powerful hands made long steady strokes. Claire projected a rare moment of vulnerability. Dimitri overheard an interchange between his hosts, a conversation that was exhaustive, measured, and supportive. He took great relief hearing laughter punctuate the discussion.

Gently taking his hand Claire asked for a moment in the garden. Their conversation was slow to start. Her words came softly as she advanced them with sheepish hesitation.

"I have dreamed of becoming a mother and I've been thinking about it more and more, I've discussed it with Ines."

"Will you adopt?" Dimitri asked.

"I had hoped to create life and to experience the blessing of being with child."

"I thought that you and Ines were…"

"Of course, yes, and she agrees. I told her of my dream, and I was hoping I could ask…" Her eyes stared at him, "forgive me if it's…"

"No, no it's, I will always be there for you – your dreams matter. I can't imagine how comfortable you'll be with me."

"Let's figure this out over the holiday, we have plenty of time."

Days of shortened sunlight brought them together for afternoons relaxing by the fire. The blazing ambers welcomed more firewood to combat the chill ushered in by the snow. They would cook for one another, retell hilarious stories while trying new things. The arrival of darkness showcased the flickering glow emanating from the hearth. The cracking sound of the wood expanding and popping was melodic drawing them closer to a meditation. Dimitri would note the graceful light of the fire complimenting the features of their faces. He wondered if they were similar in age, they must, he thought because of the unique and powerful connection he felt. Ines was close enough to dare curiosity, feel the heat of the fire, but distant enough to advance a sense of privacy. A sensual poem penned in a new physical lexicon starts slowly around the fire, an impromptu reading. It wouldn't be his last.

STRONG WINGS

HAUNTING LONELINESS WAS his primary distraction, Dimitri's thoughts remained incomplete searching for merit or syntax, at odds with his shaky afflicted pencil. Another gin and the taste of stale crackers did little to calm his strained emotions. Soulful misunderstood aspirations swirled, he wondered what calculation would clearly demonstrate when he was finished expressing a complete thought. Dimitri's disorganized perspective was elevated by boredom; completely vacant of the inspiration he sought.

Every subtle movement in the cottage was registered in a silent glance. Dimitri wished G.G.'s focus was contagious. He placed an oversized book in the center of the table using the cover as a writing tablet. Its scale projected potential brilliance and a legacy of enduring provenance. Crumbled papers of unfinished thoughts littered the floor and across the table just out of his reach.

His unanswered letter to Stephen caused him to further worry. Dimitri could guess Stephen's pending arrival would occur just as he left for the city the next morning. Another taste of warm liquor sparked the movement of his fingers. He hoped the point of his moving pencil could read his lips and make sense of the new and delightful adventures taking place in the immensity of his imagination.

Endless length
Limitless movements
Wonder meets drive
Heart finds hope
Hopeful love
Cloudless love
Growing dreams
Pure pathed approach
Carried away

Wanting her caused pain
Away and down
The west
Morning dry, morning dew
In low parts rising higher
Majestic view
Worthy of a song
No countdown
On its own
Beyond permission
Away to survive
Instinct
Freedom above all
Almost forgetting
Remembered
Twist roll and turn
In the thick of it
Gone forever

We can't
By ourselves
I keep up
Beyond all control
Contemplate immensely
And again
Propelled twice
How can we
Not hear? Whisper
Softly quenched
To know joy
To be wrong
To be willing

Devastated heart
Cold rain
Hot
Torn
Alone pulling
Pulling pulling
Away

Beyond shipwrecked, Dimitri awoke exhausted and dehydrated. His pounding head attempted to slowly lift off the table, wearily coming to rest again on a pile of papers that stuck to his ear. Feelings of guilt overcame him - he knew the answer. Progress alone was real progress delayed.

Dimitri's best intention toward improving stamina, concentration, and memory would need more support. The Center for Servicemen was his next stop; he owed it, if not to himself, to Nurse Claire and Ines. He spent a relaxing hour sipping coffee, his muted body movements challenged the rising temperature of the morning sun. He packed his gear slowly, hopeful Stephen would make an appearance.

Sister Maureen kept a pair of on-the-ready rowboats in the brush beyond her dock for discreet and easy access in and around the bay. Stephen made sure his runners and colleagues expressed their gratitude to her for her long-standing and unwavering support.

Taking a seat and positioning the oars in the oarlocks gave Dimitri a purpose, resetting something approaching goal-setting, at least for a short while. Thrusting forward he coiled his body tightly over his bent knees, his lengthy arms grabbing each weighty oar handle. One fist positioned slightly higher than the other, he exhaled deeply, pushing his feet hard to the boat's floor, as every measure of wind was forced from his lungs. He hurled his shoulders backwards flattening his body as he pulled the oar handles firmly to his throat. Exuberance invigorated his body's ceaseless motion; each splash repeated the next in a growing tempo launching him at full speed across the bay. Physical exertion and the consistent steady cadence served Dimitri well as he started to recognize tiny pieces of what he thought he should be remembering with each pull on the oars. As the bottom of the blades skimmed the water racing back to first position, each stroke moved him beyond labored agitation; jettisoning days of unrealized wellness. In each movement his arm strength met a meditation that led his body to a deeper breathing and an unblinking mental focus. He kept rowing.

LONG VIEW

H E REMEMBERED HER pale skin contrasted sharply with the bone-colored princess slip that rested smoothly on her hips. He admired the unique angle of a laced shoe with a carved French heel. The pace at which she moved made it hard for him to recount clearly, but his recollection of every small detail was getting stronger. Her laughter was endearing, sincere, and made her blush, and he couldn't forget the taste of the saltwater taffy she made him. He was puzzled at first as she reached her hand towards him.

"The taffy on your chin matches the taffy on your shoulder," she noted with a smile.

"Sadly, that's not uncommon." Stephen returned with excitement.

She licked the long sweet pull of taffy from between her fingers. With his pain and despair, Stephen was glad to have a simple memory of her that gave him tremendous joy.

In the fourteen days following Eli's death Stephen took sinful refuge in the arms of the ladies at Pinco Cheng's. The affection of Irene and Ruth extended far beyond normal customer relations. With persistence and attention, they took control of Stephen's gin and opium indulgences. They encouraged him to explore some of the newer of Cheng's eclectic menu offerings, a curiosity he wouldn't consider given his aversion to needles amid the haze of smoke. Stephen overstayed his welcome by another two weeks. Cheng's wellness incense, herbs, and teas from around the world were lost on him. The greenhouse next to Cheng's compound on the river was global and exotic, displaying Cheng's expertise and passion for all things organic. Stephen marveled at the well-tended grapes from Paso Robles, desperately trying to fill the vacant hours and distract himself from his current emotional and physical state.

When he ran out of money, he sold his boat and Cheng loaned him another hundred bucks, and when that ran out Cheng returned what was left of him to the cottage.

He smelled it first, the sinister shade of smoke on a cloudless day. The arriving blast of sunlight prevented him from opening his eyes. Half awake in the sand he could taste the salty crust on his lips, his skin was burnt and blistered. He wiped the sand fleas from his neck. His dark stiff underwear he wished would wash itself. Four days of sweating and insomnia reminded him he made it to another Wednesday morning still not sober, far from clarity.

Unable to raise his body, he struggled to lift his arms to wipe his eyes. In a blur he noticed something fuzzy and white, not a bird, a larger animal – a white cat resting higher on the beach, untouched and far from the water.

"Hi lovely," Stephen offered in the exhale of a shaky whisper.

He would later confide to Dimitri that the fuzzy blur kept just enough sanctity and hope near him to keep him out of the abyss of further self-destruction.

Outside, Stephen endured sleepless fit-filled nights, recurring one after the other. Shivering and cold, but not to be outdone by a high fever which left him completely listless.

In the darkness he almost made out the shape of what

he hoped were the outlying connecting points of a far-off constellation. If his imagination could reach above the shadow cast through the clouds and measure the brightness igniting between stars, then he could confidently exhale, reassured of his personal strength and enduring vitality. So he hoped. A celestial ruse, distracting him from the tepid hues – black hazel to another gray in an endless wave of dingy cloud formations forced on him by the cruel cluttered mistletoe of withdrawal.

Sister Maureen was the second one to find him. She came with bits of fish and hot soup that went uneaten. Maureen made contact with Cheng asking for assistance with Stephen.

"Have your girls do something," was his strident retort.

Sister Maureen's collection of resilient women didn't precisely conform as a convent by rule or approximation. They functioned together in an economy of service, and though they all yearned for faith, most were consumed by uncaring realities and circumstances without opportunity. Maureen taught them to find piety in helping others, in kitchens, and laundries for older adults. They were skilled, hardworking women who used their voice, artistry, and gracefulness to assist others. They followed Sister Maureen's directives with precision and were in constant quick-step motion. Maureen led Ana to Stephen.

Onions and fresh kale were a powerful pairing from whatever pot was boiling. He wondered who was cooking. Sister Maureen? Stephen hoped she would remember to combine anchovies with the aromatics at the right time. Was this an appetite? Stephen remained twisted in the sand, his scorched skin contorting his body in electrifying pain.

"I'm Ana, this is Aloe!"

"What? Hi, Wow that's cold!"

"That's the idea," she replied smiling, "You're badly burnt and you're coming inside today." She spread the soothing sap liberally across his shoulders.

"You know this isn't who I am or how I live," Stephen confessed with embarrassment. "This is not what I'm about, I just feel a little lost today."

"It will be okay, just stay here with me, you will get through this pretty soon." Ana reassured him. "Just stay here with me," she repeated, "you're going to be fine, just do what I say."

"How can you be sure?" he questioned with a downcast gaze.

"The word tells us to keep the faith and when you do, you can do anything you dream of – a glass half-full, if you please."

"You have water in your glass?" Stephen laughs, then coughs.

"I have unending faith in my heart" she reassures him, touching his chest.

The realization that he could almost feel a smile beginning to grace his lips and shatter the despair which handily defines his countenance, made him hopeful and inquisitive.

"Will you come again?" he wondered, turning towards her.

"Be still, I am covering these burns with more aloe"

"Were you the one cooking?"

"Yes, Sister Maureen's recipe."

"Really, the one with the anchovies? Mmm, it tastes like butterscotch!"

"Butterscotch socks – yuck!" Ana offered playfully.

It was her laughter that hooked him, an elevated feeling that was foreign and alluring followed, fueling his body when she smiled. He couldn't wait to hear her laugh again.

The constant churning of the surf lulled him back to sleep as Ana covered him in a large white sheet. He dreamed about the jousting birds, sandpipers that hopped, chasing each other on the sand bar. The beach raven with the broken feathers was relentless and the frequent winner. His physical paralysis was amplified by his emotional turmoil accented by guilt and doubt. How did the day become so divided, split in half and quartered by the tides? Was it prepared especially with the isolation he preferred in mind. He wished for the security of being alone on the sand bar, his own miniscule island, an unreachable oasis.

In a daze he whispered to himself, "I still have a lot to say, but who would listen. Would she hear?"

As the tides shifted, the last roll of a long wave disturbed his rest, a jarring attack making him anxious and feeling vulnerable about larger waves and others who travel by night.

It was that delightful scent that woke him. There was coolness on the beach. Stephen was dilapidated and hungry, half awake he could sense her arrival. She keeps speaking, and moving so quickly, Stephen felt three paces behind.

"I want to go with you, but can you translate? What?"

"You'll catch up," she boasted with confidence.

Ana's words landed quickly, and almost made sense as she brought a cup of refreshing water to his lips to start the meal. "Try this next and we can go inside," she instructed, handing him a small bowl of yesterday's soup. The warm red savory broth was medicinal; he could feel the heat and enriching nutrients.

"Savory is the newest color of the rainbow," he confirmed under his breath.

The soup ran from his chin as he drank from the bowl with both hands. He was soon distracted by a light gentle tickle on his toe. The gentle scratchy tongue of the white cat licked the toes on his right foot rolling between his legs.

"Is he yours?" Ana wondered.

"Not sure, I don't know what I have right now."

"Well, it looks like you have both of us for now, so let's get you inside," she directed.

Slowly, he moved step by step, every pace Ana took was a spring-like jolt. He found himself falling behind. His eyes watered as he looked at the sandy ground. Ana supported his left arm.

"Don't let go" Stephen pleaded.

Once they reached the small table in front of the door of the cottage, Ana covered his face and shoulders with aloe and returned to stacking the wood in an orderly pile.

"Take it easy today, I'll be by in the morning. You're getting a haircut – you'll be fine, I'll make sure of it. Goodbye."

As she darted off, Stephen's body felt a spark of excitement. Where was she from? Where was she going? Who taught her how to swing an ax? He wished she walked slower so he could ask her, and so he could keep watching her walk away. He looked out over the dune towards his former resting spot anticipating her return. He felt a sense of progress as he sat wrapped in a sand free blanket and felt the breeze. He dozed off, wondering how she got to Sister Maureen's house every day. Daybreak brought a jarring morning aloe greeting, it was cold and soothing, but at least she would laugh at his reaction. After four days of aloe and restorative care, he found himself sitting in the bay. Ana sat on the low dock above him working a pair of scissors.

When he looked up at her the color in her eyes morphed into a brilliant layered palate of aqua to azure. The sun and sparkle came back together as each iris reflected the bay in front of them. In the moment he forgot about where the courage to be confident again came from, and where it had been.

She sat above him cutting the long curls of his hair with his shoulders resting between her knees. He was able to sit, walk, and stand the early successes of a longer recovery. The sunshine felt different around Ana, it didn't burn and it wasn't hot. He could feel it from inside. It was bright and rather kind, like the first giggle that had led to a larger laugh.

The nectar from the fresh berries she gave him burst and tickled his mouth. The cool shallow water failed to temper the deep longing he felt as he imagined the passion of the succulent kiss they would share and the dizzying blissful feeling that would follow. In some cultures they would be married. The flavors of the black and currant berries were an intense sweet contrast to the salt and dehydration of the days prior. The joyful explosion sweetly wore through the briny plaque that covered his mouth. Playfully he bit into another berry coating the juicy pulp across both lips granting them a new and reinvigorated vitality. He entertained folly, splashing as he spun his arms in circle wondering how to remain completely aimless in the bay for the next four days. The half-life of unrealized ambition he thought, in a moment of self-deprecation. Eight days to fail again and feel shame he assured himself of doom and deeper doubt.

"Who would listen? Who would hear?" he whispered.

At least he had time to reset, to identify and locate a part of a healthier persona that would guide him to his much unrealized potential. He was seeing more in motion around him, and it was exciting. The shadow rolled across the blossoms near the cottage as the clouds shifted. Her skin was a light source, radiant. All he could do was stare as she stood in the flimsy and underbuilt enclosure of the outdoor shower. Through the mystery of steam above her he could see the pointed rhythm of her fingers as she washed her hair. He walked slowly toward the bay to give the appearance of respect for her privacy. As his health, strength and constitution recovered, so did his appetite. He welcomed the depth of feelings, but couldn't stand the devilish draw and harsh lust-filled yearning that made him stare at her. His confusion grew as he found new urges among reverence.

Her unfamiliar song that he wouldn't remember was a breathtaking Irish blessing that stopped him in his tracks, what other glorious surprises did Ana possess? Laying back in the warm salt water of the bay, he held a plump blackberry between his lips. He felt his heart race for the first time in months and firmly understood that beyond his pulse was the rest of his renewed self. Could he add the hues of her lips? A new color to his evolving rainbow? Stephen was eager to reach the bounty of a joyous life, but he must protect Ana from his increasing brawny desire. He was determined to embrace an elevated standard that Eli would have rejected. He watched Ana dart towards the point, she was beyond worthy. Was he ready? How would she view him? Stephen's distracted mind guided and pulled him to his last layer of respectability.

His needs, amid isolation, and testosterone made her the subject of greater asks. A handwritten note would eventually reach Maureen asking that Ana be reassigned. He included a letter expressing his gratitude to Ana, highlighted by cash he borrowed to compensate her for her efforts.

It was painful loneliness that followed in the days ahead. He could sense vitality near the point. He spent his waking hours lost, thinking of her, clinging to his untempered desire, so close to discovery and self-abandonment. His soul was grieving for someone who was still alive, a curious dirge for a fading heartbeat. She was still near, just beyond the point. He stepped into the bay, the water was cool as it passed his ankle. The splash on the back of his knee reminded him of the aloe that was cold and healing. He stopped when the water reached mid-thigh. He looked behind, and then ahead falling to his knees and completely submerging himself into the water. A baptismal offering of renewal and hope to jettison short-comings and reset his out-of-balanced emotions. As he stood up he wiped the water from his face and reluctantly turned back to the point restoring Ana's virtuous prospects and regard for her future. Stephen spent the evening by the fire dreaming of Ana's embrace. He would pretend to hug her at length and dare her not to let go.

"Whoever lets go first, loses!" he mused.

He smiled imagining the sound of her infectious laughter. It was the first few smiles in a long time and the realization that his grief for Ana leaving was countervailed by the despair of losing his friend, Eli. He would never forget or completely understand everything she did for him in such a short amount of time. It was an intense struggle not to picture her with him in every quiet moment. He would think of her often and remember her blushing fondly.

SAINT MALO

N O LONGER BEING with him, her imagination made smooth every flaw Dimitri may have had. Fabienne created a smarter, wiser, truer cast of him. It made it easier to feel his touch as she dreamed about the curl of his lips, and his towering regal stance, yes – regal and solid driven by his sturdy frame as she imagined them moving rhythmically.

Each gentle step whisked her deeper into a lush daydream. She felt protected. Surrounding the walled city was a smooth expanse of wet sand abandoned by the tides that seemed to stretch to the horizon. The narrow Rue Sainte-Ann was just as Eli had described. Three wooden benches met at a turn across from the Saint-Vincent Cathedral of Saint Malo. Fabienne admired the non-stop tiny Elena urgently chatting to a collection of flowers blooming across from where they were seated.

"She will tend to a beautiful garden one day, won't you my love?" Veronique asserted.

"Henri, stay close, don't run off. Father Louis will ask for us to join him after the service is over," Fabienne instructed.

"I am so thankful he convinced us to make this trip, it's been a joy to decompress, take a break and see something new. This ocean air is so restorative. I demand to hear more about your recipe for the prized cailles, I will beg for details next Fabienne, you should come to the café. If you're interested we could do it together. I'm open early for breakfast and the rest, but if you have a notion of expanding to a late lunch or supper we have access to all the farms and local hunters," Veronique offered.

Fabienne marveled at the stained glass that retold grand stories of exploration and mindful risk that challenged destiny and fortune. A plaque blessed the spot where the seafaring travelers departed. Faith lunged from the square and narrow streets propelling the vaulted sanctuary to new heights. Sturdy blocks of granite formed grand arches as beams of warm light filled the chapel contrasting with mysterious anomalies of darker spaces. She smiled hearing Henri sing to the young Elena.

"We really should do it," Fabienne confirmed.

An elegant rumble of the chorus seemed to shake the oversized doors wide open. Father Louis' sermon elevated the 1535 history of the chapel, his offering of faith flowed through to the congregants reaching all assembled. He positioned himself just beyond the doorframe to offer a hug or firm hand on a shoulder of all who exited the church.

"The lord is still making miracles, and they apply to each one of you," Father Louis promised walking toward the benches.

"Veronique and Fabienne, what a joy it is to see you both, and come children, let me see you. Let's walk this way we have the perfect place right here."

Father Louis led them past curved windows and doorframes to a neighborhood bistro. The dining area reached outside through open windows that extended to the ceiling. Father Louis would find his seat after stopping to say hello to a handful of guests.

"Have you considered asking her? She should give it her full attention. I'm going to be here alternating months, but will be looking forward to seeing you victorious and grow. I hope you'll do it together."

Henri and Elena pulled on Father Louis' arm urging him to take part in their playful performance that was about to commence.

"How adorable are both of you? I can't thank you enough for making this trip. You should join me here in the future. You both and the lovely children will always be welcome near the rectory. The apartment for visitors is quite comfortable and hopelessly under-used," Father Louis offered.

"Veronique has been generous to extend the idea of a new prospect and my participation at the café," Fabienne explained with a smile.

"I'm looking for the perfect recipe for cailles," Veronique expressed with determination. She imagined a swirling marinade with aromatics and peppercorns.

"Perfect," Father Louis' voice was higher, "I will leave you two, I have to prepare for our second service. I can save you a seat in the first pew."

"Father, thank you," Veronique and Fabienne both extended a hand towards him. Elena and Henri held his flowing sleeve as he turned to exit.

"Lovely and joyful," he said walking away, "you both carry the spirit of the Lord."

"I'm excited for his success," Veronique said looking at the menu. She then changed the subject.

"I know you miss Dimitri, I miss Eli."

"Of course Dimitri is bright in my heart," Fabienne explained. "I went to Ines after it happened. She brought a lovely material to me to fashion a dress for Nurse Claire, a celebration of their last patient, I guess. I had to see him. She told me what Nurse Claire had said, he couldn't remember much of the past, but I insisted, it was so painful. I tried and tried, then went again. I offered to help nurse him, he thought I was Ines at one point. He was there for months, Nurse Claire said he may never regain the memory of the past, but had made phenomenal progress. She told me familiar streets and the boat home would position him for further recovery. He landed at a center for servicemen, near an aunt and her family. I will miss Dimitri, but I am thankful for the time we shared, especially the love he and Sam offered to Henri and I. Blessings truly. And Father Louis is determined to see you successful."

"Us successful!" Veronique replied, "Dimitri has been rather generous toward Nurse Claire and Ines, she won't take a penny. She has directed everything he sends her to Father Louis' efforts and this support has reached Elena. I am humbled and reverent when we speak of him."

LASTING SCARS

IN THE MORNING he hated people, by evening he hated everything else. Disdain and darkness were the first emotions to find him when he awoke. He was anxious, still in a daze when he called for her.

"God damn it Lily," Carter barked, "get here now and tell someone to bring coffee and a hot towel."

Lily couldn't reconcile their matrimonial discord with the personal effort she put forth striving to reclaim and project a harmonious front amid the severed bond between them.

"How did you sleep?" Lily asked sheepishly.

"With all that snoring. I'm heading to my meeting, the whole day is gonna be wasted with that fool lawyer."

It was a dusting of powder and certain positioning of her hair that met the layers of her dress, appointed, pressed, and crisp. Her morning was consumed with details and preparations for lunch with Carter that he would, by the sounds of things, miss. She was rushing to another lonely meal. Her isolation stirred feelings, bright and worried. She noted how perfect the small vase of fresh cut flowers was, placing her head in her hand and quietly thinking about how she could change her marriage. Carter invited her for the season, to be with him and be supportive, what was different? She couldn't see it. A solitary tear flowed down her cheek attesting to her emotional confession, a physical recognition of the hidden dilemma that was senseless and torturous. Lily leaned back positioning her eyes in view of the narrow doorframe.

"Thank you Walter. So good," she said, moving the items on the plate. It wasn't a lie, the food was delicious, but Lily had no appetite.

"Ma'am, another note from your unmet pen pal, Marie." Walter said extending an envelope to Lily.

"So thoughtful, right?" Lily was genuinely excited by the attention, "you read it Walter. Carter made it clear for me to stay away, not sure why?"

"She's extending an open invitation and wants to be available if you're looking to enter into the regional social circles. I've met her and her staff, they have been wonderful neighbors and they seem tightly connected to things beyond themselves," he continued reading. "She assures her ranch is open to you for any occasion – she promises, and looks forward to your visit."

"Thanks again, Walter." Lily said, carefully refolding her napkin then heading to the stairs.

"Yes, Ma'am."

The moment he said those words her professional staff urgently started preparations for dinner. When staff flowed from house to home within the same family it resulted in a more lasting and supportive working relationship.

Upstairs, solitude brought contemplation. She tried to highlight the virtue of having independence in her letters home, but the tortured reality of abuse dampened the impact of her words. She would keep writing. She dropped her stack of envelopes when she heard the engine of the Dodge Brother 30 getting louder. The slam of the door told her she was expected downstairs. Carter hurled a volley of obscenities and directives aimed at reorganizing the efforts of his outside staff.

Carter was unmoved from his chair on the veranda.

"Ice!" he ordered.

Walter was moving quickly.

"Just forget it already," Carter barked vaulting the crystal tumbler hard to the patio floor.

Lily ran from inside, asking, "Is everything alright?"

"No, damn it, get this mess cleaned up." Carter insisted.

"What on earth?" Lily mumbled under her breath.

"What did you say? Pick it up."

"Okay." She knelt reaching for the broken pieces.

"Now!" Carter demanded.

The side table became an extension of his fist hurling towards Lily. Her face and forearm caught the brunt of the force, the momentum knocking her completely to the ground.

"Stop your damn crying and pick up that glass." Carter raged.

The history of her relationship and the building blocks of the foundation of her life to this moment flashed before her eyes. Cascading resentment, anger, and fear countervailed any notion of connection between them. Shards of broken crystal cut deeper than normal glass, stabbing her as she knelt on the slate floor. She felt Carter's hands grab her shoulders. The sheer force of her dress being pulled and ripped left her hog-tied, bound by this maniac's diabolical grip. Her arms were locked in fabric at her elbows; his force left her under garments in tatters at her feet.

"Stop this!" Lily screeched.

"Don't you say a word to me."

His right hand pulled her hair once and again farther

down raising her chin, as his left hand grabbed her throat tightly.

"You pathetic bitch, I should kill you," he promised.

Lily fought desperately trying to free herself. Carter's punch landed hard in the eye.

"Sir! Sir! Stop this at once," Walter demanded, racing to the veranda.

"Mind your business." Carter told him, tossing her aside.

"Get her out of my sight."

Every cut on her bare feet reinforced how demonic and unhinged he had become in such a short period of time.

Carter's motor started and headed down the drive. Lily's fingers picked at the points of broken glass as she hid behind a large sofa.

"Ma' am, can I arrange a car or ring a doctor for you?"

"I'm leaving. Now!"

"Shall I pack you a bag? Perfume?"

"I can't wait, and you should go too. I will contact my father, just protect yourself - and thank you, he could have killed me."

She wondered; would he follow her? Would he come back?

Lily wiped her feet once more and swiftly dashed out the front door, stumbling down the long drive.

A PROMISE

THE RELENTLESS POUNDING on the door startled Marie's chambermaid who tossed her linens on the nearest chair and raced from the kitchen. Slightly ajar, the open door almost offered an invitation. Lily's eyes met hers then quickly looked away.

"Come in child, come inside and let me look at you," she said, urgently swinging the door wide-open. "You're bleeding and whoever hit you, knew what they were doing. Shame dear. Don't worry I will fix you up. Stay still. Let me get a bandage and some water. When did you eat last?"

Her gracious question went unanswered. Lily's beaten and weary forehead fell softly resting on a small round cushion. The flow of adrenaline that propelled Lily out of her home and down the lane to Marie's front hall, had left her body. A trail of blood stained the dainty pillow extending down to the floor.

"O'dear, let me see this cut. You are safe here," the chambermaid said calmly. "Marie will make sure of it. She's at the ranch house, I will bring you to her later, just rest a while and I'll find you a clean skirt and fresh blouse. And give me those muddy shoes."

The dust and dirt of the long driveway had taken a toll.

"I have clothes and my belongings are being packed there, I just can't go back – never ever."

Lily's words ushered forth an onset of tears that emerged from the corner of her eyes. Her elbows and her clenched fists accented her declaration, landing hard on the sofa. Nauseous and out of breath she surrendered to emotional turmoil realizing that for the first time in her life she was without a home.

"I will have one of the team make that a quick errand today, now rest. We will take good care of you. Tell me your name?"

A low struggled whisper offered "Lily." She was asleep shortly thereafter. The curtains were quietly drawn, a thin slice of sunlight flickered through a sliver in the tall window treatment, the narrow curtain extended from floor to ceiling. The deep plush fabric was accented by a sheer white underlayer that would by wind and time press its way through the curtains. Twisting in and out of the light, the orchestral tempest grew, swirling and dancing eventually landing on the armrest next to Lily. When her eyes opened she was confused by the darkness, and unsure of exactly where she was, it took a moment of worry to recall.

Her large suitcases and round leather hatboxes had all been collected, and neatly assembled, staged on the shadow side of the porch. A valise was placed next to her which contained personal items; soaps, perfume, jewelry and a hidden panel concealing an envelope of cash given to her by her father.

Lily's dad, Roth, had immense instincts that would now, she realized be confirmed as omnipotent. The added shock of disappointing parental expectations was an additional scratch to her soul, a weight she didn't need to bear. Roth had given his blessing and supported the marriage looking past his doubts in order to honor Lily's wishes. The evolving strain of her relationship with Carter had the unintended consequence of bringing Roth closer to Lily. As frustrated as she was with her current predicament, she took great comfort knowing she could lean heavily on her father.

The short nap didn't do much to heal, it just gave her bruises and injuries time to find a deeper and more focused pain. She limped as she walked to the bathroom where she would wash herself from head to toe with a hand towel, slowly freshening up for the drive across the estate to meet her new host, Marie. A graceful motor arrived to usher Lily through the unique landscape and orchards of Marie's vast enterprise. Her guide was unaware of exactly how distant she was from present concerns as he drove her past every landmark on the grounds. Lily relived her escape over and over again in her mind. Each step she took was a faster pace to freedom leading her to Marie's sanctuary. Every pace stripped away weeks of abuse and neglect from Carter. She shook her head wondering how often she had prayed for the strength to liberate herself. The courage and determination it took to turn the doorknob and flee was new, unrefined and raw. She would add hopeful resurrection to her piety.

He continued, describing the grouse and pheasants that made the long grasses in the meadow their home. The speed of the car would move ever slowly so as not to startle the precious bevy. Lily's attitude was beginning to reset, their long dramatic feathers were a fantasy of hues and color. The smooth ivory seat was sturdy and comfortable as the ground bounced the pair down the lane. As they moved closer to the edge of the long expansive meadow, Lily noted an orchard of almond trees as far as the eye could see. Fire crimson leaves with yellow accents carpeted the entrance. Waves of undulating long bent grass welcomed the blanket of the weightless falling leaves. The late afternoon sun tore through remaining leaves on the branches, an eruption of color and bursting light. Looking backwards over her shoulder she noticed a stubborn brown leaf, slightly red in color, unwilling to fall or surrender to the ground. She admired its purpose and determination to challenge gravity and define one's own destiny.

The orchard was a natural boundary encircling the front house, horse stable and presentation rink. A wide porch flowed generously from the front steps around both sides of the structure. The expanse was a comfortable outdoor space capped with oversized ceiling fans interconnected by cables, cooling and offering enough moving air to keep the space free of gnats and other distractions.

It was her boots Lily noticed first. They were a texture and fashion she had never seen. She wore a personal armor, black and sturdy serving function, but interestingly elegant at the same time. Long flowing necklaces extended beyond wide shoulder padding, landing on a leather breastplate.

"My name is Lily," she announced stepping down out of the auto.

Marie moved closer in.

"I expected you, only sooner, call me Marie," she said just above a whisper. "You have a lonely resiliency lingering somewhere deep inside your heart. You're safe here and know that my men don't accommodate uninvited callers."

"But I..."

"I knew you would find us, I just didn't know when."

Marie glanced toward Alejandro, her lead rancher, who seemed to glide, surrounding the two women.

"My team will protect you, and so will I," she pledged to the young woman. Lily felt an outpouring of emotion and relief, an audible sigh was heard as she wiped her tears. Her new ally directed her to a small table in the corner of the patio.

"Those trees are breathtaking..." Lily paused startled by the grandeur of the orchard.

"Lovely, right, you should make the time to see them blossom, the flowers are exquisite," Marie explained.

From her chair against the side of the railing she could sense the power of a large saddled horse untied, standing motionless beneath a tree. Its color mirrored Marie's wardrobe with wisps of grey highlights. Lily was unsure where they came from. A valet brought a tray of ice water with lemon slices to the table. Lily examined the details of Marie's accessories up close. Handcrafted silver buttons served as jewelry to adorn the multitude of black layers Marie wore.

"Make yourself at home, you're welcome here. I've had Kennor send for some of your concerns."

"But if Carter sees me, he could be violent," Lily worried.

"No, no – stop it. Leave that to me, no one can harm you now." Marie's hand touched Lily's shoulder.

"Let me show you around." She instructed, walking Lily to the oversized horse.

"Step on this," Marie instructed Lily; she mounted the saddle on the horse raising her to a vaulted and stately elevation. "Ali has everything you will need, I made sure you have plenty of clothes. We will ride early in the morning, I will find you."

"I'm just afraid to be on my own horse," Lily confessed.

"Good, then it's a plan! We'll have a great start, I will help you."

Marie walked the horse and Lily around the property showing her the barn, and equestrian rink. She ended the tour at a small home adjacent to the rink. The guesthouse had two bedrooms, a small kitchen and a fireplace.

"How did you know?"

"We all knew what a terror he has been, and he has toyed with trouble for too long. Now it has gone too far. I'm sorry my dear. There is more to it, but that is for dinner tonight. Change, we are informal, meet by the outdoor fire just before dusk."

The large fire offered warmth, ambiance, and served as the kitchen and staging area for a table set for ten. Marie preferred to be outside in the elements and under the stars. She wore a black fabric cape, adorned with ornate roping that detailed the edges. Hosting came naturally to Marie, and in short order, Lily was not just among the group, she was an integral part of it. Lily was enraptured by the flair of the evening, the alluring Argentinian cuisine, and hearing different languages spoken – she didn't want the night to end. The table began to clear as Marie asked Lily to join her by the fire. The sip of bourbon Marie shared was a shock to Lily's sweet mouth, with a gasp she spit the devilish mixture into the fire.

"Carter is unhinged. The whiskey has a deep hold on him. Tonight he is in Almera, it's a short ride from here."

"How do you know this?" Lily asked.

"Just listen, my team has been aware of the violence in these homes for some time." Marie expected Lily's next question.

"Homes?"

"Families." Marie delivered the news bluntly and directly.

"What?!" Prove this now Lily's eyes implored.

"It's true, he has another woman and child. His father has just recently learned about this situation," Marie offered with pained empathy.

"Sadly, his violence has reached them too – we will help them both. Should he harm them or you, or if this continues, I will change things. Sometimes things need to be ended, not like in a game of chess."

Marie was earnest, "I know Walter was instructed to close the house. So you will stay with us, thank you."

Lily was breathing hard. Her chest was pounding, she was worried now for not just herself, but wondered about these new others, were they family too?

Marie's gait had the sound of a horseman as she turned to the porch. Lily admired her rugged strength and wondered how she fashioned such graceful layers and feminine riding clothes. The bedroom in the small house was perfectly safe. Lily silently listened to the ambers of the fire as they died down. She laid in the center of the bed, leaving the sheets and blankets undisturbed. She had imposed enough for one day, she thought, as she drifted to sleep. Her old companion, insomnia would visit her shortly thereafter.

Lily was up and about early; Marie arrived with two horses minutes later. She instructed Alejandro to place the parcels by the door and to leave the horses in her care.

"Good morning," Lily offered joyously excited to see her breath in the cool air, "What is this?"

"Put these on, they are for you." Marie thrust two bags and a hat box into her hands.

"You shouldn't have, that is much too generous."

"Boots, something warm and a hat, you'll need all three, let's go," Marie commanded.

Lily opened the first bag and found a pair of low boots wrapped in paper that was in a language she couldn't discern or understand. The riding hat held a wide brim and a woven lariat to hang comfortably from around her neck. In the last parcel was a large, black-striped poncho suited to drape over her fitted clothes beneath.

"You look perfect, and that will keep you warm and dry. Now take this."

Marie gracefully opened her long coat, showcasing the length of her legs and the ornate straps of her boots. She untied a leather pouch removing a small silver dagger. With both hands Marie offered it to Lily.

"Take this with you, I pray you will never need it. When I am with you, I will be dead before you need to reach for it - now let's go."

The morning ride took the pair to a vista overlooking the almond tree orchards where they could almost see the main house far off in the distance.

"We'll camp here."

"What?" Lily asked.

"You'll learn to love it. I asked Alejandro to drop off supplies for this evening; we'll find some firewood, tend to the horses and prepare to cook. It will be a crystal clear night."

When they returned from gathering wood, two large baskets were left at camp. Poultry and a melody of vegetables were on hand, Marie reached for a bottle of wine first, then the questioning began.

"Are you a farmer? Are you related to Alejandro? Why are you being so generous to me? Forgive me, I really am so appreciative." Lily expressed sincerely.

"Hand me those glasses, let's toast to another glorious evening. Yes, I farm and hold land among other interests. Alejandro is family as are the others. We're not really cousins, but we are connected. They have always been loyal and I offer the truest form of the same. Let me show you how to make a fire."

Lily's hands naturally fit the shape of the branches and logs they collected near the edge of the rows of trees. Each action was intentional and deliberate. Marie placed each rock and cut log in its right place. Lily paid close attention. The warmth added to the experience, another simple element layered on the one before. Deliciously basic meals accented by quality, flavor and feeling. Lily found a new comfort being with Marie. It was stimulating to be outdoors and learning how to be on one's own.

"I was always told what I couldn't do. That what was proper would prevent me from what I had hoped to do. Or it would need a chaperone or escort, and look at me now," Lily announced beaming.

"I grant you freedom and independence," Marie assured Lily, wrapping her arm around her shoulders.

"I hope you continue to shape your life through your passions. Create your path, have goals, yes, of course, but chase your dreams wildly."

Marie was artful at helping her to discover an elevated self-worth, and along the way, Lily learned how to make time for herself, find peace with who she was, and make her dreams a priority. Self-esteem married a gracious confidence, the result of which transformed her mental outlook and give her a steady posture, a louder laugh and a wider smile.

Their excursions continued and absent from the daily ride was any mention of Carter and the pain that she had put behind her. In the month that had passed Marie would continue to confide in Lily, leading to a confession.

"I'm telling you this just not to have anything lingering or creating division – we tell each other everything, nothing comes between us, ever. So, and yes a bit of a confession, if I was able to feel shame, anyway, some years ago I had a short time with Carter. I should have told you sooner."

Laughing, Lily placed her arm firmly around Marie's shoulder, "You poor thing, come and stay with me, I'll protect you. Such joy in mutual despair."

Their laughter continued as they hugged. Somehow Lily had evolved into a proud member of the team in dress, language, and interest. She found it stimulating and exotic to be near. Her change in approach didn't need to be a straight line, she would find a way to be emotionally and physically rebuilt. Their conversation was interrupted by the arrival of Marie's ranch hand Guillermo, who offered Lily a lingering stare. Lily didn't blink or look away.

"That degree of mutual flirtation with young men and women will lead to passionate lovemaking, young lady," Marie teased.

Their laughter grew. Guillermo worked outside, his body awash with sweat, but never overly so. He was always dressed appropriately for any occasion even when working with a machine or animal. His aftershave was unique and hinted of gasoline. He was a hand to Marie because he knew how to get things done. He gave her a second stare. Lily was flattered. She was completely blushing, she wiped her face, now flush with tears.

"Thanks Guillermo, show Lily how good you work with your hands, the baskets are by the fire. Are you hungry? There's some chicken leftover, help yourself. You can show my friend how you use your mouth."

Marie always knew when candor cut. The pair continued to laugh at Guillermo's expense. Lily made a point to rub his shoulder to show her genuine appreciation and interest. Resurrected.

WITHOUT CARTER

CHANGES COME, BUT not soon enough to stem the years of violence and abuse. Self-absorbed drunkenness led to the calamity responsible for the death of the parents of two young children. The wanton inertia of his speeding truck was merciless as it crashed through the window of the luncheonette. The handwritten police report, blood stained from the amount of broken glass, noted the careless driver laughing uncontrollably as he regained consciousness. Carter thought the reach of his powerful family would insulate him from scrutiny and any serious legal issue. The Sumter County Magistrate took exception sentencing him to treatment and medical confinement for ten years. Carter's dad paid the hefty fine.

His isolated home confinement came to a jarring and abrupt end complete with handcuffs and a sheriff's escort. Deep sandy ruts flanked both sides of the road leading to the asylum. Four half dead trees lined the walkway as a one-legged blackbird flew under a low ceiling of dark clouds. Five chipped stoned steps capped with a broken etched glass lantern welcomed the drunken Carter, who stumbled in a stupor through the last door he would ever enter.

An unimpressed glance welcomed him. "You can have a seat, we'll be right with you," the receptionist directed.

"Listen hon, you might not know – I'm Carter, and I won't be staying too long. So, get the Doctor or whoever is in charge, now. I need to reach my family in New York, you've heard of them, right?"

"Of course I have, we've been expecting you." Carter didn't notice the two orderlies approaching from behind or the nurse with the syringe who served an ample sedative swiftly into his shoulder.

"Call my dad," was Carter's last unanswered directive as he collapsed in the chair.

"Doc. said not to make too much fuss over him, don't think he's aiming for a Nobel Prize."

He found himself almost awake ten hours later. Dazed, Carter was physically unable to inquire or respond, anxiousness and concern were new for him.

He lay comatose as the straps tightened around his chest, legs, and arms. They were tightened even further until the strap pinched the last quarter inch of flesh before hitting the bone. When he fully came to, he forgave himself quickly, never worrying about the past. An ego-centric approach to an abundant and endlessly fortunate future that wouldn't last. His first treatment was scheduled for the late afternoon. Muscle relaxers would have helped prevent the seizure that was massive and unexpected. The current of the heavy-handed electric shock therapy was too much to bear. Carter died two days sober, but not as sober as the justice of the peace who directed him to the treatment center. The severity of the seizure was noted in the medical record filed with the death certificate. In death Carter wasn't even an afterthought, he was now an anonymous, inaccurate typo-laden form that would be filed away and forgotten. No loved ones, no discerning anguish - the squeaky wheel of the bed rolling down the hall was the only unique feature left of his irrelevant existence. The specimen was removed to an oversized shower area in the mortuary on the second floor. Six gurneys stained with blood and vomit masked the excrement that inspired the larceny that was about to take place. Rubber gloves, a mask and an apron reaching the floor were all needed to clean and prepare his thin prematurely aged body for burial.

The orderly extinguished his second consecutive cigarette snapping the silver case closed, half-opened, and then slamming it closed again. An elegant cursive "C" was prominently engraved on the front of the case announcing prior ownership and assuring that the contents were premium. His swift hands glided in and out of Carter's possessions replacing rings, a watch, and chain with throwaway trinkets to not draw attention to his mortuary self-enrichment. He moved next to Carter's sweater, coat, as well as his luggage, and every pocket was searched. His elaborate sleight of hand continued as Alejandro arrived. An overwhelming dose of stale smoke permeated the room. Lanky fingers squeezed the tip of his cigarette with a precise fold.

"Hey, got a light? This was worth it. Thank her for me will you? Seriously, thank her please."

Alejandro said nothing, offering a reassuring smile. Carter's open mouth was filled completely with the contents of a small bucket, a swirl of active maggots; whose numbers would only multiply in the sealed casket combined with the southern heat on the journey north. He would be disfigured beyond recognition eternally stripped of his dashing countenance he traded on for most of his life. A final thank you and fateful retaliation, robbing his family of an open casket and a dignified memorial.

Alejandro extended his hand delivering a fold of cash to his accomplice.

"You'll thank her, right?"

The doctor knew the judge who told him about the calls from Washington D.C. and Carter's father asking for understanding. His disappointment in the loss of a patient was short-lived. He delivered the news to the court by letter explaining the inconsistent result and the experimental nature of Carter's treatment. The Doctor's explanation was a bookend to a grievous chapter universally accepted as sad, yet with a necessary outcome. Most were glad to see the issue behind them.

• • •

Marie seldom had the inclination or the time to let her guard down, but with her friend the judge it was different, they would share a toast to justice served over a private luncheon, their joined hands would linger. Sincerity and gratitude moved to joyous and welcome laughter and bountiful stories Marie would then interject to announce her plan and commitment.

"In the near term, I will tend to the Almera mother and child. I will also contact the family and remind them of one's moral obligations."

Marie was direct, forceful to the point of dominance with an iron grip, leaving her friend free to make fewer decisions and remove the robe. Their unpinned magnetism and building tempest found force and new direction with every kiss tuning the pace of their afternoon embrace to a liberated and perfectly salacious rendezvous. Confined energy released distracted them from the sunburst leaves and branches that filled the second-floor window with brilliant beams of refracted light. As the late sunset faded warm lanterns showcased the smooth cobblestone pathways that framed the quiet square below them. Marie chose the climatic moment to hurl her arms overhead reaching high above, falling back naked across the length of the oversized couch. Boots and blouses complimented the pile of clothes strung from the chair, cascading to the floor. Marie knew what she wanted and used both hands to reassert control.

• • •

Back at home, Lily came to cherish her weekend excursions shared with her childhood friend, Amelia. Fresh air and quality time discussing common interests were capped with areas of structure and support for Lily. Amelia noted the muted piece of her natural curiosity had become something near confident, elevated, yet, not quite vibrant. Her pensive outlook had found a touch of originality and a more exuberant spirit. Amelia used the time on the ferry across the Hudson River to search for a spark of her oldest and dearest friend, she could sense it just beyond Lily's properly polished veneer. Amelia would start right away - a simple introduction could be transformational. She pondered who would be the right connection? She knew the right one would prove meaningful. Amelia rejected the idea of Lily not being ready and it was time to jettison the pitiful, mindful soft-spoken approaches.

The journey home gave Amelia ample time to seriously consider who would be right or a near match for Lily. Amelia was tickled, feeling like a big sister again. She was joyous at the prospect for mentoring and seeing Lily reborn. A light kiss was a goodbye that they both knew wasn't, but rather a "till tomorrow." Lily's calm arrival would soon recoil.

Sad eyes greeted Lily as she stepped into her father's parlor.

"Lily, come sit with me. I have a piece of terrible news." He stepped forward and put his arm around her.

"Daddy are you alright?" she asked.

"I have word from down south. Apparently Carter has died suddenly following a medical procedure gone wrong," her father said slowly.

When his words landed Lily was steady, though she knew that there was still room for loss, and it could continue to expand. She was home, she had moved on, she felt the power of her family's embrace and was ever thankful for her father's and Amelia's unending love for her.

LIGHTNING STRIKE

THE MORNING STROLL followed a cup of strong black coffee that gave their legs and spirits a lift. The rising temperature would bring a heat and a midday burn shortly that would urgently require them to find shade.

The dancing breeze and warmth swirled past Lily as they turned the corner toward the bay. The short corset cover that Lily was wearing stopped mid-thigh. It was just enough covering to feel appropriately dressed, and just sheer enough to feel every measure of a soothing wind, no matter how soft. The water was inviting as they walked into the almost still water of the bay. Lily dragged her toe in the sand, as if to close the circle.

The water was warm and clear, with the sand underneath pleasantly rippled. Dimitri took her finger and pulled her deeper into the water. Lily reached and hugged his neck as they sank together in the shallow water.

"Woohoo this does feel wonderful," she said, and then suddenly added, "Look!" as she pointed at a school of shiny fish.

"Oh yes, those little beauties won't hurt us," Dimitri said.

"They're lovely, truly lovely and everywhere," Lily was enraptured.

"They will stay nearby all morning, but they won't bother you," Dimitri reassured her.

"They sparkle," Lily noted.

"Right, but that's the problem," Dimitri explained, "if you're going to swim with a school of sparkly fish, you have to look out for a larger fish. There is always a larger fish."

"Where?" She exclaimed, looking intensely at the water.

"Always good to keep an eye out, some of these bigger fellas have teeth, but I've never been bitten. They would like you though, with those long legs, and little toes, like berries, yum!" he teased.

Dimitri slid his feet closer to Lily.

"Stop," Lily begged looking at the sandy bottom of the bay.

"Eli and I used to joke about being in the food chain swimming in the bay, there's always a bigger fish. It's a good life and business lesson on who you swim with, choose wisely!"

"Amen."

Lily knelt down letting the soothing water roll over her shoulders and hair over her forehead and down her face. She would hand stand, and bounce among the shiny little ones. Were these fish covered in scales or diamonds and silver? she mused. Dimitri kept watch like a lifeguard no big fish would dare get close.

Coming up she coughed, laughed, and cleared the water running from her nose.

"Very elegant!" Dimitri announced.

"You have no idea," she smiled.

Watching her swim he saw how playful, how youthful, bursting with creativity she was. Every step was a dance, a story. Crystal clear water flowed down her arms as she lifted them above her head. The cool coating created by the flow of water made her sparkle in the sunlight, as if she were a sculpture of glass standing before him. He took a step forward and lifted her up, drawing her closer to him. He cradled her above the water, holding her close, kissing her lips, and caressing her breast. He wouldn't mention or describe the large brown fish that scared away the shiny school.

As her toes left the sand she raised her chin and laughed, her arms wrapped around his neck. Her heart was full of joy, she felt complete. He kissed her again, and she kissed him holding his lips in hers starting the game. She burst to the path dancing toward the cottage, he had no chance of catching her. Lily was winded when she reached the tiny backyard. She placed her hands on her knees, breathing deeply to catch her breath. The wet, white, shear slip that almost passed for clothes was an afterthought. Lily knew she was almost naked in the yard, and it didn't bother her for a second. As her hand reached for the last touch of the seam of her slip, Dimitri's hand swallowed hers and started lifting it over her head.

A cool splash rinsed her in a new wave of falling water, flowing down her back. The moisture on her skin touched the air giving her a chill. Lily's hand combed Dimitri's hair as he draped her slip over the clothesline. She tagged him with a quick firm smack on his ass, starting the chase to the front of the house. Dashing through the door, she sat on the small wooden bench next to the table, smiling and panting.

He was late.

"Hey, that smarts," he said.

He stood in front of her after the race inside. His hand touched her shoulder as he laughed, as he tried to catch his breath. He leaned over her, and her forehead touched him just above his belly button. Lily kept her head in place as water dripped from her wet hair flowing down his body.

She slowly moved her hands, resting them low, against his hip, he couldn't see her smiling, but she was playful and loving. Dimitri was out of the sun, relaxed. His fishing plans could wait.

Lily tugged his still wet bathing shorts lower, first to his thigh, and again to his knees and then to the floor. His legs were muscular, so removing his wet shorts required determination and strength. She laughed as he kicked them aside. She looked up at him and gently kissed a taut angled muscle that made his waist rock hard. Her fingernails on her right hand teased the back of Dimitri's left leg grazing his butt, coming to rest high on the back of his leg. Her left hand pressed firmly into his right hip. He was quiet and still. Lily brought her face close and wrapped her lips around his near mouth-filling erection. She took all of him in, slowly at first, causing him to moan, inhale and shake. Lily moved rhythmically, forward and farther, again and again. Her hands, unmoved, held firm; for a moment she felt control and could sense Dimitri's anticipation growing. He touched her hair and held her head, which she shook away. Moving briskly, back and forth, she paused, daring to create urgency, she continued swallowing and breathing. Lily's mind again wandered as she moved again and again. A drop of sweat rolled down her shoulder along her breast, landing on her thigh, causing her to refocus, keying back into the beat of her playful rhythm. The motion of her tongue swirled in a whirlwind at his tip and actively on his length, and edges to tease Dimitri, she stopped once more to heighten his tension. She felt an explosive release was near as his body began to rock and his breathing turned to low growls. The early arrival of his urgent offering was met with the gasp of a cough followed by laughter, she paused, but wouldn't completely stop until his body shuddered one last time and he touched her shoulder. Out of breath, he tried to step back to sit in the chair. The sweat that held her hands in place, practically glued them to his body, she gently peeled them from his skin. Lily stood up and walked into the kitchen to find a small washcloth to wipe her mouth, chin and breasts. The coarse dry fibers of cotton tickled her skin. Lily could taste the salt on her breath and the sea in the air.

"You're so good to me, but I'm not done," he panted softly, smiling, trying to pull her on top of him.

"Oh, really?" she smiled, certain he was kidding.

The two were motionless on the sofa, still, feeling drained by the heat of the day. He fell asleep first, his body like a sun-roasted oven. Lily couldn't fight the warmth that radiated as she used his chest as a firm pillow and rested her arms around his shoulders. His breathing in and out, slowly rocked her to sleep.

The touch of soft footprints moving around the front door got Lily's attention enough to listen, but not open her eyes. How long was she asleep? It was a deep sleep, no dreams, just a restorative nap. She slowly shook her head. Was someone outside? Lily quietly got up and walked in the rear bedroom and pulled a light dress quickly over her head to cover her newly tanned skin. She tiptoed gently toward the door and when she looked up she saw G.G., the white cat, trotting on a low wall made of dark stone. She turned back and grabbed a large worn hat hanging by the door.

"Well let's have a walk," she said smiling.

The dark wall was a coarse, long barrier that stood between the plant life on the natural sand dune and the patio on the front of the house. Lily followed G.G., who had stopped to stand a post in a corner formed by the wall.

G.G.'s intense stare looked up and out, beyond a destination. He was always on duty; his ears were equally attentive. G.G. was a worthy sentry in any context. He naturally took the posture of command a regal leader, versed in chivalry and adored by all.

At the wall's end the path over the dune was on the left and down the path to the right led to the bay. G.G. purred.

"Hi sweetheart, how's your day going?" Lily got closer.

G.G. burst ahead just as Lily got within two steps.

"Don't worry, my friend, I appreciate and fully understand the no touching policy on your island. Exactly how did you get here by the way?"

Lily realized that the question she asked was an overarching question. She was now taking a hike and it was still hot, even though the sun wasn't directly overhead. Every step on the island felt new. She quietly relished this adventure and the company of G.G. her explorer-guide. Her five-minute stroll with G.G. took her around the curved point that set out into the ocean. She could hear the crashing waves from a tiny almost imperceptible cove far below her. The island rose higher, and she knew new she was almost on top of the bluffs that Stephen had pointed out to her as she steered the boat to the dock. G.G. was always in eyesight, ten feet ahead, looking back every few paces as if to tease her and draw her closer to their journey's end.

Lily walked among the bushes that created a deep thicket that overgrew the trail. Her tender feet insisted she place them with care as she jumped and danced over the sharp pine needles and random branches that lay in her path. As the route curved, she saw G.G. hop and run up a rocky step that would cause Lily to use her hands and feet to climb as she followed.

She threw her leg to the right and used her hands to pull her body up. It took a second to stand up and see all of the long vast meadow.

"Well, you really do spoil me! I thought for certain we were walking in circles. How lovely!"

High above the water, standing in a breeze, Lily stepped into a majestic meadow bursting with wild flowers. Her radiant smile instantly became a wide open-mouthed gasp that she would cover with both hands. Excitement and unanticipated temptation took hold. She had to have more of this, urgently. Lily exuberantly became part of the landscape, she stepped forward wiping a tear from her cheek. Her hands touched the small blossoms of shear pink, ruby red, and tiny goldenrod. Swirling monarch butterflies surprised other resting butterflies in a dance, taking place between her knees. She would remember the exact shade and hues to describe to Dimitri. He would come and paint this field, he would have to, she just knew. Facing north she could feel the heat of the sun landing on her shoulders, from the west she was surrounded by a peaceful wind and a vibrant melody of color. G.G. bellowed a low meow that got Lily's attention. Lily had already picked and placed a small blossom in her hair.

"Thank you G.G. this is an enchanting delight."

Lily's body enjoyed the fresh air, while the meadow launched a gentle fragrance into the wind. G.G. kept moving forward.

"Where are you going? You don't want to miss these stunning flowers, Angel!" she shouted.

She followed her feline friend deeper in the meadow, then farther uphill, around curves, downhill and up again. The pines gave her shade. She could see parts of the bay and hear the waves landing against the rocks, far below to her left. The cottage was out of sight as she looked to the east, and the field she was in led to another undiscovered oasis.

From the top of the bluff, she followed G.G. downhill with a natural view that would be the perfect place to watch the sunset. G.G. was almost invisible, but the movement of the plants with her white fur helped Lily's searching eyes. Small whistling birds darted from the tall grass ahead of them. G.G. leaped into a rocky area that defined the edge of a tree line.

The downhill slope was easy on her legs, and each step flopped in the tall grass. She realized she would have to walk uphill on the way home. Lily started to hear the movement of water. On one side of her was a line of trees, the beginning of a beautiful and majestic forest, standing in a shallow pool of water with thick green branches covered with dotted small cones. She moved in the opposite direction, walking towards the sound of a flowing brook. At the edge of the meadow, she moved just a few paces further under the canopy of the new forest and found herself standing on large flat rocks with a brook that cut between them.

"Well this feels like home!"

Lily slowly walked over to the brook and smiled, placing her tired feet in the cool refreshing water. G.G. called out and Lily looked over her shoulder to the left. Towering over her was a rocky peak.

Lily continued to carry on the one-way conversation with her feline friend. "You really are something special, thank you for sharing this. It's so beautiful."

Lily walked slowly, climbed down, and took care to watch her steps. At the bottom she marveled at the serene waterfall. It was taller than Dimitri and she tried to guess exactly how high it stood. She put her hand in the water and brought it to her lips.

"Ooh, Yes!"

The water was cool, clear and tasted like spring, her lips were coated in minerals. Lily was confident and comfortable, completely embraced by the pines. She quickly raised her skirt over her head and stood pure in the brook. She used her hands to drink water and moved to the waterfall finding a seat at its base. A chill restored her overheated body to a soothing temperature the instant her skin touched the water. She was thankful for the needed hydration and the quiet moment to bathe her body as she sat on the warm smooth rock.

What else did this Eden possess? she wondered.

Nothing, she imagined, could ever surpass the experience - a sea of flowers to infinity, and a natural spring bursting with a graceful waterfall.

In the shade surrounded by cool water, Lily wondered about Amelia, her family, and if they ever knew this level of happiness and urgent bliss? She would write Amelia, this joy wasn't to be contained in polite, soft-spoken pleasantries that veiled the essence and spirit in her heart. Her mind was calm and her soul refreshed. She allowed herself a number of extended minutes of serene peace and quiet, and then reset the clock. With her eyes closed she gave thanks and prayed that her friends and family could understand for themselves the feeling of renewal that was flowing through her being, enlivened her soul. Grace.

"G.G.?" The cat was gone.

Lily carried her dress and placed the large hat on her head as her naked body flowed through the string of meadows. The sun dried her deeply tanned skin. Leaving the meadow her feet found sand. Lily pulled her dress over her head and left the buttons open. Her wet hair started to dry as the cottage came into sight.

"The sun suits you. Your hair is turning a softer sort of ruby color, what color is that? Where did you go?" Dimitri asked.

"I have seen the most enchanting part of the island!"

"Really, the most enchanting place on the island, on God's green earth, is right here. Please note the shrimp and corn - and you're with me!"

He gave her a hug.

"Seriously, where did you go?"

"Past the meadows above the hill, there is a stream with a lovely waterfall, with fresh water."

"Right, Eli told me about that one day while we where fishing. I tried to find it and got lost. I got hot, lost, and tired."

"Follow G.G. he understands distance and location, it was so lovely. A brilliant field of wild flowers and tall grasses," Lily explained.

Hearing this his eyes opened wide.

"Really? Will you show me in the morning? Eli was a little brief on the details. It sounds like something..."

"It's something you have to see," Lily interrupted, "you'll want to paint this landscape, it's stunning."

"I'm going to cook some, no, all of this. Have a sip and relax a bit," he said, handing her a cup.

Lily wiped her feet off and slipped on thinly soled fabric shoes. It was more like a dancer's slipper that was gently worn in, but it was perfect in the stiff grass that covered the yard.

Dimitri boiled a cauldron of salted water, adding aromatic spices and thin slices of root vegetables, just as Ines and his Aunt Renee would have suggested. The corn followed, and near the end, he would add the shrimp, clams, and mussels he had caught in the bay.

"There was a small cove that I could see from a cliff, have you ever gone in there?"

"Only with Stephen, once. It's very dangerous if the tide is against you, the waves and rocks are merciless on a small boat. Stephen knows that cove well. I'm sure he uses it to store - no hide - whatever he is moving. Makes sense, since it's dark, remote, cool, perfect warehousing, I'd guess."

Pouring more scotch into the small coffee cup, which they sipped and shared, Lily went to work peeling shrimp as the corn cooled down. The liquor burned in her throat, as her eyes widened. She coughed and covered her smiling mouth.

A single flame flickered and danced in a handheld oil lantern.

"I have an idea that's just got me out of my mind, I think it could be a wonderful experience for Amelia, I'd like to invite her to come out for a night or two. What do you think?"

"Sure, brilliant idea, when? I remember when I first met her, after Sunday services, we spoke about painting as a way to keep my hands and mind focused. I suggested she sit for me at the studio, which must have been completely forward of me. She told me she is hopelessly shy, but that her friend Lily would be perfect for the canvas. She told me how beautiful you were and that the painting would be radiant, and she wasn't wrong. I kind of feel like I owe her a debt of gratitude for introducing us and for everything she's done at the center. It'd be nice to spend some more time getting to know her. She can share the bed with you, I'll sleep on the sofa or pass out by the fire."

"I think she would love it here, and it would be a nice break from her businesses and family concerns"

"Write her a note, pick a date and time for Stephen to meet her at the pier."

"Just Super!" she said, throwing her arms around him.

They spent the rest of the evening in a deep conversation, full of fresh seafood and more wine then spirits, their effortless laughter flowed. The weightless sun slowly drifted lower, and the sunset was muted by rain and a distant storm.

The evening chill urged Lily to toss two small logs on the fire. She could feel the brisk wind of an approaching storm. The sun of the day had drained every ounce of energy out of her. It wasn't long before Lily headed to the bedroom, she couldn't resist any longer. Lying down, she reached for the hardcover book next to her bed. She was hopeful for a few more pages of the unexpected adventures of a red fox, but eventually, the graceful sound of the waves pulled her gently to a needed rest.

Dimitri sat alone on the porch, his thoughts oscillating between where he was in his life and the expectations that were ingrained in him by the lessons and powerful example of his aunt. Was it guilt that tugged on the underpinning of his conscience? His anxiousness faded with another sip. His knew his self-doubt came from inactivity and lack of focus. He regarded himself at his best when he was looking forward towards the next opportunity for prosperity or service. He listened to his companion, G.G. and smiled to himself, realizing he had not accounted for the profound presence of Lily in his heart and life.

Dimitri smiled, feeling a bit tipsy, noticing that the breeze had turned to full wind and he tried to get some rest. Half in a dream, Dimitri could sense the hours pass, as the restless wind filled the bedroom.

When the lightning strike hit the tree adjacent to the

cottage, it crashed to the ground with an earth-shaking explosion. The cottage shook and shifted. The rage that followed propelled Lily to the floor. Dimitri vaulted from the bed and burst through the bedroom door naked, grabbing his bayonet by the front door. Lily saw his hand was holding his knife high, and he was racing toward the water, determined, and screaming orders. Petrified, still, by the side of the bed looking out the window into the darkness, her lungs gasped, searching for air. Fear and adrenaline combined overtaking the movement of her body. She could only see him in the distance when lightning flashed.

Was he going to kill something? Did he know he could kill? In his mind he was at war, clearly. Could she run? Would he harm her? Quietly in the dark, she used her hands to guide herself as she moved through the adjacent rooms to the rear door, into the yard and down the long path. She was instantly soaked, her body shivered, the scratching of rain cutting sharply in the chill. She raced to the dock, and tied the rope to a pillar with hopes of signaling Stephen at daybreak. The thunder and lighting fired and flashed. Lily cried, as her wet lace top clung to her cold quivering skin. She knelt by the dock to stay unseen, thinking for a minute, trying to understand what was happening. Was she in danger? Could she hide? Petrified and sobbing, rain poured from her hair down her body. Could she stay? She considered swimming into the bay but to where? Would he harm himself? Lighting and thunder kept rolling overhead, but had moved eastward across the expanse of the island.

G.G. cried out in the storm, and again loudly, piercing her soul. Lily was tortured wondering where the sound came from, lost in panic she made a mad dash up the path. Lily covered the dune and was on the beach in a few seconds though it felt like forever. Out of breath and in a cold sweat, she could see him below her on the beach, face down in the sand with his arms spread wide apart.

"Dimitri, Dimitri!"

He didn't move. The tempo of the rain started to soften as Lily on her knees, reached out to touch him.

"O' Dimitri, tell me you're okay?"

She touched his sandy wet hair.

"Huh? You're soaking wet" he wondered. A few seconds passed.

"How did we get here? Are you okay?"

"Are you? What happened?" She could feel her pounding heart starting to slow.

"It was a nightmare, I ran them back, I think." Dimitri was unclear and worried about what had just happened.

"I know, you want to – maybe we should talk about it?" Lily offered.

"Yeah, but later."

Dimitri moved slowly, he could see white in a blur as he rubbed his eyes. He thrust himself forward to lift himself up.

Lily picked up the oversized blade and the pair walked slowly up the dune to put Dimitri back in bed. Seeing the broken door fragments that remained, Dimitri mused "I don't suppose you did that?"

His sullen eyes aimed downward, he was concerned and worried, but he did his best to project a steady mind.

"Don't be frightened Lily, I will never hurt you"

Dimitri towel-dried himself and got back into bed. Lily slowly caressed his arms with her fingers as he fell asleep.

In the quiet, gentle rain, wind, and darkness that night, the pain became real. Same sad story was becoming her specialty. She could grow to hate love and the sting of watery eyes, or she could keep true to her instincts. This was where she knew she was needed. This was where she belonged.

She exhaled softly and slowly got out of bed. She walked quietly out of the back door, heading down the moonlit path toward the dock in the cool predawn breeze. She felt a reassuring calm. With confident ease she untied the rope hanging on the pillar and placed it in its original position.

BAPTISMAL WIND

"**O**F COURSE THE breeze."

"I'm sorry, I didn't mean to be impertinent," Lily offered lowering her gaze.

"That's quite alright, you're lovely my dear," Sister Maureen replied putting Lily at ease.

The dryness of her thin skin jarred Lily as Sister Maureen's hand reached toward her. Her touch was gritty and void of any moisture.

"I am self-absorbed they tell me," Sister Maureen explained with laughter "distant, and completely incompatible in any personal relationships, except for Hal. He's my salvation, and the wind has become a source of sanctuary."

"I feel that way too, I mean about finding sanctuary and finding peace, not about Hal, I mean," Lily revealed.

"It's a rarity, and at times a gift, to be reminded of God's grace knowing we are present, surrounded by these vast and rich blessings," Sister Maureen replied, pausing to look far beyond the horizon. Quietly, she elevated this sandy point to an hallowed chapel. Lily needed no confessional, but the guilt of being unchurched made her more determined than ever to make faith a priority in her life.

There was a tremendous amount of work ahead of her, and Lily knew Sister Maureen could not envision what was in store or how vast her plans would be for the point. So her questions continued; how often would Maureen hold a service, how large would the ideal chapel be? The altar Dimitri could repair, perhaps? They would require hymnal books, bibles and proper pews.

Sister Maureen described officiating at a funeral for a fisherman that was held on the island at church point a few years prior. Friends of the departed gathered for prayer, song and reflection, followed by an interment in the modest graveyard near Maureen's cottage that was over the water across from the point, almost visible to those in the pews. Hal tends to the plot.

She was forthcoming in describing having to leave the Church, admitting her imperfect walk of faith with the Lord, amid an unintended scandal that reached her Order, a decade prior. Lily was forgiving, hoping her new friend would share her faith and knowledge to those on the water, in what she hoped would be bible study and a new community of faith embracing all.

Lily's list of projects continued in her mind; Altar pieces? Vestments? Sacred vessels? What else would be needed to complete the altar, and reach an elevated state of sanctuary?

Sister Maureen extended both hands to say goodbye, her eyes wishing her new ally well. A charm on her bracelet rang softly – an abbreviated peal, announcing her departure. Leaving the new church, Sister Maureen followed a narrow path that guided her through the protective trees by the waters edge, a short rowboat ride away from her nearby cottage.

Lily sat on the handcrafted bench made of birch wood, quietly admiring the height of the cedar and birch trees on the point that gave it solitude. Her next project was less of a challenge, dragging a collection of branches down the center aisle past the pews to a bonfire spot on the beach. In a few moments the renovation began, the main areas were swept clear of debris and pine needles. Looking skyward she could see the high branches swaying in the ocean air, but in the pews, she was enveloped in a calm serenity. Across the circle of trees, she noticed G.G. propped on a thin branch licking her feet in a ray of sunshine.

"Hello G.G.," she called crossing in the circle. Curiously, G.G. didn't dash away. Lily made her way past the bushes, almost making it within arms length before G.G. jumped off the branch, landing on the tilted side of a low, half-buried wooden cupboard. G.G. maintained the status quo of feline isolation by leaping again to the sand and darting to the other side of the pews. Lily didn't know what to make of this discovery, what it was or to whom it belonged. She wiped the sand from around the weathered door. As she pulled it open, the chest revealed a large flat wooden case and a thick book of hymns. Time was less kind to the pages of the book than the wooden case. Opening the box, a sparkle of sunlight reflected in the ornate metal illuminating her face. An oversized silver plate, engraved and covered in details accompanied a small matching cup for wine, adorned with biblical filigree. The set rested in a dark chiffon fabric, which she thought would be perfect for a tablecloth. She turned to share the news and return proper accolades to her guide, but as expected G.G. had moved on. She would certainly need Dimitri's help to unearth the chest, and she wondered what other treasures may lay undiscovered just below the sand.

Lily carefully returned G.G.'s faithful treasures back to the cupboard, and took one last turn around the circle between the rows of pews; first position, second...Lily darted back to the cottage to tell Dimitri what had happened. She was completely confident amidst this stand of trees, with reverence and hard work, she and Sister Maureen could create an unofficial church of the great outdoors, bringing faith back to the point and into their lives.

Dimitri's afternoon was less purposed. His nap was framed by an oversized white sheet, fresh from the line having been dried in the warm sunshine. He wore a tight linen shirt and shorts reaching mid-thigh. He lay half awake as G.G. crossed over his feet. G.G.'s white, pure as the driven snow coat hinted dingy gray against the background of the artic white sheet. Lily's dramatic arrival met him with a complete ecart en l'air.

"Wow, I didn't know you could do that, and so well."

Lily turned thrice with precision, spotting, extended her flowing ballerina arms, bowed, and came to a towering resting position.

"Brava, you're smart, leave them asking for more."

Lily circled the sheet en pointe, her mind floating, upheld by the memory and melody of a lonesome violin. The sensual offering continued as she opened her arms to him. Her focus and longing movements hinted of Scheherazade at the Ballet Russes. At just the right moment she urgently found the perfect point of entry, swooping low next to Dimitri thrusting her torso forward and back.

"And Sister Maureen understands what's possible, but we need your help. And I found...well, G.G. found a chest with an antique plate in a wooden case, who do you think it belonged to?"

Dimitri sat up, trying to remember the history of the point to conjure a logical explanation.

"I betcha it goes back years. The point is the entrance to

the bay, a natural meeting place for generations. So calm and really peaceful down there. Eli's uncle never went to church, so I don't think he would have known anything about it.

"You need my help? How heavy is it?" he asked with a teasing grin.

"I knew you would, but seriously thank you. It's just heavy enough," she laughingly assured.

Pockets of air under the sheet cushioned her body as she rolled herself next to him, her head coming to rest softly on his arm. A steady crash of rolling waves was muted by a row of high dunes and softened further by the sway of tall sea grass. She felt like she could reach, if she tried, to touch and hold the mesmerizing clouds that passed high overhead. Looking up beyond the first cirrus layer she counted nine birds, wings extended, motionless as they gracefully traveled. Their unmoved outstretched wings required no exertion. Was this their natural resting position? It seemed the birds had to be in formation or at least near each other in an array, instinctually drawn together, even when they didn't understand why. She wondered the same, and questioned how they traveled so far and remained so powerfully interconnected across such a vast distance in a simple clear sky? The aloft collective challenged the philosophy of positivism stretching empirical laws to an explanation resting firmly in a faith-driven, yet undetermined realm.

A relaxing warm breeze blanketed the pair as they clung to one another allowing them to drift into a deep slumber. A slight shift in temperature gently woke them a few hours later, as the sky moved from shadow to dusk. Barely awake, she didn't notice it at first.

A serendipitous transformation was underway, the beams

and rays of the generous sunset burst into the small yard creating a dazzling display of lights. The rose-colored oasis embraced them from head to toe. Dimitri's white sheet took on the color of a new auburn flag, ushering a unique persona designed by the warm tones of the setting sun. In the last moments of the evening, a new ruby castle formed from the cottage allowing them to take command of the island, and the surrounding environs. An elegant sovereign nation lovingly crafted for just two inhabitants in the illustrious imagination of two seafaring artisans propelled by faith and beauty, void of conflict or strife. Lily was enraptured, her focus moved from the ghostly dandelion seeds delicately sliding through the air around her, to the flashing of fireflies from deep within dark green bushes.

"Not everyone sees this," Dimitri softly offered.

His open hand guided her, vaulting her directly into the heart of this majestic and ethereal orchestration. Her wide-eyes recognized it in an instant: the sky in his painting, the cottage was illuminated in a sunburst of crimson. Breathless and silent the pair stood mesmerized, pleasantly adrift in this bountiful offering from Mother Nature.

Dimitri turned walking slowly toward the door, his body was stiff, and his arms were burnt by the sun. He lit a candle in the kitchen, poured a cup of wine. He smiled, intent on convincing Lily that the best way to handle an uneven tan was to lie naked in the sun the very next day. Lily's dance continued into the cottage toward the bedroom, she emerged wearing one of Dimitri's sleeveless undershirts revealing her lean body, and long legs. In the yard beyond the window he could see the last touch of the blushing sky. Lily's dark hair held the disappearing highlights of the sun.

"I have a sunbathing plan to propose for tomorrow"

"I have more urgent plans for you tonight," she declared as she reached for him.

"Did you try this?" he asked, handing her a warm bowl of seafood chowder, "it's perfection."

The two spoke softly as the light of the candle became stronger as the sunlight dimmed completely.

"I haven't found a poem that expresses the depth of the affinity we share, but I'm willing to keep looking."

"A loving affinity," she corrected him. "Keep looking or start writing," she smiled, sliding a writing set in the center of the table closer to him.

"A loving affinity, that certainly has a ring to it."

As soon as the whisper of the word "ring" left his lips, he anxiously wondered if it had just advanced a matrimonial signal into their hearts.

"It certainly does, I can't wait to see what sort of inspired soliloquy you come up with," Lily laughingly replied, poking her finger into his chest.

SHE FLED

THE SCENT OF flowers overpowered Lily as she fled the crowded hall. The next wave of humidity caught her with a blast as she left. Out through the doorway, into the sunlight, the oppressive heat quickly covered her dry, soft skin with moisture. Heading north, her step off the cobblestone curb allowed a cool swift breeze to lift the flap of her confident, unusually short dress. She blushed, a smile and liberating moment of laughter followed, driving her faster down the middle of the empty street. Her arms relaxed, falling to her side as if to capture the last grasps of wind that filled her dress. She was alive with light and air, the setting sun covering her in warmth and color. The direct sun wasn't alone in revealing her shape to the world around her, the brisk movement of her step offered it. Proudly marching, not to escape the rising temperature, but to find all of it.

"Well hello!"

Looking to her left, she stopped abruptly, as their eyes met. How did Dimitri always find her?

"This is a surprise." She couldn't stand her jittery excitement and was unable to mask her growing smile.

A few short steps and it started. Their arms touched first, intertwined and a laugh pulled them closer together. He gently touched her face and moved her hair off the right side of her cheek. Her eyes found his, and when they did, their lips met.

Silently, connecting, pulling closer and closer, their locked embrace lasted until the last beams of heavenly light stretched a shadow across the length of the darkening street. The pair was still. Short movements, quick breaths and a pounding chest, kept the two unaware and not caring about onlookers or the surroundings. She wondered to herself, was this belligerent? Commitment? Or just what passion felt like? With another kiss she had her answer, and fell deeply, back into the middle of the moment.

A question following his greeting was their beginning: Do you remember this? His hand moved from his pocket, placing a small piece of sea coral in hers. Her fingers naturally played the rough tiny piece.

"Let's go back," said Lily hopefully.

"I am already packed," Dimitri answered.

"I don't need anything more than what I have on," she assured.

Lily's tug on his left arm drew him closer, with both hands. She pulled, urgently, and removed any feelings of doubt between them. As she walked she leaned her shoulder forward, pressing her body against his, heightening the unexpressed physical bond that connected them.

Dusk turned darker along the cobblestone. The curve in the lane insulated them from the exhibition that just passed, and the exhilarating optimistic future that was unknown, and alluring. The anonymity she felt accelerated her step. She wasn't alone - just free, no, liberated, confident and above the gaze of scrutiny.

A light floral note fell softly from the flower boxes overhead, a welcome contrast from the distinct city air.

The curved wall guided them as Lily clung to Dimitri's arm. Looking down she saw the century old stone that would usually sully the precious shoes that carried her. Sleek, and wrapped in the perfect embrace, she cherished each effortless step of what was more than an easy stroll.

WITH HEART

"WELCOME SIR!" THE eager doorman announced with urgency. Eighteen dollars worth of a newly tailored suit with a fresh collar, paired with a shine, buys entrée and status, however misplaced, Dimitri thought. He tried to keep his breathing measured and to keep a presence of calm that would support his words with reassurance of meaning and thoughtfulness.

He seldom had the opportunity to wear this suit, his most expensive of the two he owned. He wore it to events of celebration and weddings - appropriate given today's mission and planned conversation. His other suit he kept covered in dark fabric in a secluded closet in a room he almost never entered, and wouldn't even look at it unless the unthinkable had happened. The two were remarkably similar, the latter a tone darker for solemn funerary functions. Sadly, he thought, he always had a dark suit ready.

He had never met Lily's father and knew very little about him, his family or his work. A quick lift to the 16th floor and Dimitri was transported to a different world. The doors opened to the loud chatter of an open room, full of people, bent over large tables covered in designs and plans of buildings and streetscapes.

He was quickly greeted by a sharp and fashionable staff member.

"You must be my 11a.m., Amelia told me you would be the dashing one!" She rested her hand on his arm. "I'm Evelyn, Mr. Roth's private secretary," she said.

"Hi, you're very kind, I'm Dimitri, thanks for finding a few minutes for me."

In two glances, Dimitri noted her short blond hair and the curls that flowed to her ears and a refreshing fragrant smell that surrounded her. It was a stark contrast to the cigar smoke that filled parts of the floor.

"Just follow me through here and we're just across the hall," she continued.

Dimitri's eyes kept track of Evelyn's tall slender frame as she seemed to glide towards their destination.

The sound of her heels shifted from the clack on the wood floor of the work area to muted steps in the carpeted area. The sound of the open room disappeared as he was funneled down the narrow hall into a quiet office. Every few minutes the occasional shout followed by a demur reply broke the silence.

"Just a couple ahead of you, I will let him know you're here. Can I get you anything?" Evelyn asked. "If you need anything at all, you know where to find me."

"Thank you, that's very kind of you," Dimitri said taking a seat away from the two other groups waiting to have their meetings.

Dimitri was seated on a long pew covered with a deep ruby padded cushion. The place had a regal feeling about it; that signaled to the faint hearted, don't waste time. To the right were four blurry panels of glass that let a small amount of light fall on the bench. An oversized wood cabinet separated him from the rest of the room. The intimate dimly lit space seemed to protect him from sparks and rage coming from the heated retorts in the other room. Evelyn worked a telephone while another gentleman walked in and out bringing messages and letters to her.

Dimitri used his time to gather his thoughts and quiet his heart with the hope of expressing his sincerest of intentions to Lily's father. Two businessmen left the inner office saying few words and looking at the floor. As they exited, Dimitri would hear one man raise his voice and chastise the other for misguided comments in the meeting that just ended.

Evelyn apologized for the next meeting that was running into its second hour. He spent his time listening to the movements of a large ceiling fan struggling to cool the room. A small breeze came through an open window just behind Evelyn's desk. The combination of the two dampened the cigar smoke that filled the office. The long wait allowed Dimitri to jettison any anxious feeling he had when he first arrived. He thought about how Lily would take the news. One-way or another he would bring joy or pain. He was ready, confident and needed the doors to open.

"Dimitri! Come on in, sorry to keep you waiting. These fellows are just clearing out."

The departing businessmen moved with haste, picking up papers, with the hope of clearing off the large wooden table in time for Mr. Roth's next conversation. His large fireplace was surrounded by huge, framed renderings showcasing building details on all the walls. A small fire crackled illuminating the deep green rug beneath them.

"Can I get you anything?" Mr. Roth offered Dimitri, "Eve!"

"No, but thank you. It's a pleasure to meet you, I appreciate you taking the time to meet with me."

"Nonsense, anytime. Have a seat. Any friend of Amelia's, I'm happy to make myself available for, she said it was important to her."

"And me too sir." Dimitri took his seat.

"You see sir, Lily and I have been together, well, dating for some time and I thought it was appropriate to introduce myself."

Mr. Roth rested his forearms on the wooden table and leaned forward, staring at Dimitri.

"I didn't want you to find out about us in a conversation with others. The complete reason for my reaching out to you is that Lily and I are in love."

"I see," he said, as his stare and volume intensified.

"My hope is that we will be able to make our affections and my, well, our intentions clear," he confessed. "I'd like your blessing. I would like your support to help make our relationship successful. I aim to make Lily my wife." Dimitri's body twitched, reacting to those few words finally being uttered out loud and to another person.

"I see. And how will you live? Suppose you'll need some resources to make a home?" Lily's father inquired.

"I'm not asking for anything other than your permission and the hope you'll be supportive. We'll make you proud," Dimitri proclaimed.

"She got herself in a jam with the last fella, sounds like she's on the spot?"

"No, no, not at all. No pressure, and not a circumstance to mention, none at all," Dimitri's candor seemed to resonate.

"But, to your question, I'm part of a small trading company, and I have a modest, but growing real estate concern," he continued.

"Good for you. I have what some call a giant real estate empire, we should talk, I'd love to hear how you do it. Are you a landlord? You leveraged to be in the markets?" Mr. Roth asked.

"Yes, I have half a block in town with three buildings and thirty sandy acres over the bay." Dimitri replied somewhat surprised by his complete answer.

"I've heard they want to preserve some of those lands, not sure how that affects you. It'll likely keep it quiet out there. I was approached by some folks hoping to keep the barrier islands strictly for animals and preservation," Mr. Roth replied.

"I'm not in the stock market yet," Dimitri assured him, "and I have no margins or debts. I tend to invest in things I can see and touch and people I believe in."

"Smart. Perhaps not, time will tell. I am seeing a number of people do quite well in the markets, we'll see. Feels a bit like a race, but with large sums of money. What kind of square footage do you have? What kind of height? You can go higher on your own, but if the blocks connect, and you connect the right investors, you could really have growth potential. The future of this town is vertical. I've also heard of plans to build on wetlands that are filled in, to build around the edges. Amelia speaks highly of you she mentioned you were in the service and you're helping with her center. You look like you're doing well and you survived the horrors over there?" Mr. Roth inquired.

"I'm doing a bit better than some. You're right, the center is going to help with the transition for so many of the boys. I'm also trying to help Amelia with whatever support I can give."

"Amelia's opinion carries a lot of weight with me. You

certainly seem more solid than the last fella, well." Mr. Roth looked downward.

"Lily's the happiest she has ever been, that's a fact. I am too. I didn't tell her I was coming," Dimitri confided.

"Son, say no more," Mr. Roth said taking a deep breath. "I will keep your confidence, I'm glad that the two of you have found each other and you are upheld by good friends like Amelia, it's good to have a few of those around. It's clear you're on your way, but if you need a hand, find me directly. I will do everything possible to see you both succeed. Thank you for coming to see me, you did this the right way. You both will have to come to lunch, have Lily phone, and bring Amelia. Keep me abreast of your plans." And then, surprisingly, "Welcome to the family."

Dimitri fought back a tear, stood and shook Lily's father's extended hand. His other hand landed firmly on Dimitri's shoulder. A short conversation and a pat on the back and it was done, he did it. His life would be forever changed for the better, he was certain.

"Eve, Cigar!"

"Yes, sir," she said walking Dimitri to the door.

"Evelyn, thanks again," Dimitri said.

"Bye for now, and congrats, that seemed to go quite well," she whispered.

Evelyn scanned the office and locked the outer door, she returned to the inner office and closed the door behind her. She bit the rounded end of a cigar and extended it to Mr. Roth who slowly placed it between his lips.

"Exciting times Eve," he mumbled as he lit the cigar.

She circled behind his chair, letting her hand move across his shoulders. She paused before she emptied the ashtray into the fireplace.

"He seems thoughtful, and boy, he is striking."

Mr. Roth slid his left hand around her tiny waist, resting below her belt, a place that was not unfamiliar to him. It started with a light embrace. "She deserves only good things," he said optimistically, looking up at her.

"The afternoon schedule," Evelyn offered with a smile, "is free and clear." Her body signaled a purposeful longing as she deliberately moved closer.

When she returned to her desk, she took a moment to check her hair, repositioning a small four-prong wooden pin eloquently in a curl on the right side, just above her ear. She adjusted her blouse and dress as she reached for a small square piece of stationery stacked on a tray. Her dainty fingers wrote in cursive what could only be described as graceful, three words: Clear Skies, Eve. She closed the envelope and wrote the name Amelia on the front. She turned it over, lit a match, and melted a piece of taupe colored wax over the seam. Her ring, a family heirloom, made the impression with its coat-of-arms.

Evelyn left the outer office.

"Charles, please take this to Amelia's Center for Servicemen at once."

"Yes ma'am," and her attendant was gone.

HEART STRINGS

OF THE MANY stately homes on the Palisades, Lyncrest is a property of noted distinction whose history and elegance nurtured a vibrant legacy that flowed generationally. Unlike the others, the family seemed to gravitate to certain areas of the home. The kitchen served as the common area, a small dining area expanded participation. The other larger rooms were held for formal events.

A rare misstep caught Amelia's toe on her way in, she didn't understand the coarse gravel that welcomed her through the back entrance into the kitchen. Roth showered in diamonds she would have to urge him to find a more suitable hardscape.

"Scraped my shoes, you really…ROTH? What in the world?" she exclaimed.

"Come join, these oysters won't shuck themselves."

"Where's Tad?" she asked, noticing Roth's perfectly tailored suit. "Let me help?"

"Open that white, and pour yourself a glass," he ordered, pointing with his chin. "My hands are wet and I'm really getting the hang of this. Tad's girlfriend is having a baby, just went into labor. He ran out leaving the roast and the oysters to me, so exciting."

"Ms. Roth?" Amelia inquired politely.

"Not here. She's taking Flagler's railroad to Palm Beach, staying more than the season apparently." His shift in tone told a fuller story and his puppy dog eyes said a bit more. "I manage a great deal of things," he confessed, "but I can't seem to control one or two turbulent heart strings."

"So sorry to hear Roth," she moved closer touching his elbow. "If you ever need a host I'm happy to fill in. You poor thing."

"I will definitely take you up on that next time I have a proper event. And with Tad out I may need to come by. Today, I have invited a special guest, Evelyn, who is arriving shortly," Roth offered with a smile.

"Hurrah, I can't wait to see her."

"So, how is my Amelia?" he asked.

"Okay, kinda," her body language led to Roth's protective reply.

"Out with it."

"It's Dad," she admitted, "he's just stubborn."

"Is that all?" Roth questioned.

"Stubborn and frustrating. I run a damn good meeting, and I run a tight ship," Amelia explained.

"I know, that why I want you to leave all the family business behind and come work with me."

"I direct things, efficiently, with large profits and returns – consistently," she continued.

"So I hear." Roth confirmed.

"Dad's still the face of the company, but it's my ship," she continued.

"So what's the issue? Roth asked. "Lots of men haven't done business with women, their loss. My life wouldn't function with our Eve, and your family wouldn't function without you."

"Dad's hanging on to legacy and loyalty plays from decades ago. Old favors long past paid, and he won't consider changing, year after year."

"Generosity and loyalty, quite the crime. Option two is let it go, it will be expensive, but it keeps him content. It's all about perception and relevance – his word on the street and in the markets," Roth explained.

"And that's the other thing. You want some of this?" she offered reaching for a glass. "We are diversified. Not one market, different sectors, little risk – I appreciate he came up with a wink and a nod and all that, but he can't stop, even at his age. He can't stop looking over his shoulder," Amelia continued.

"I'd offer to chat with him, but you know his answer, the cost of doing business. You really should consider running my business. You and my Evelyn are the smartest people I know. That's her!" Roth exclaimed.

Roth stopped handling the oysters and quickly washed his hands, his head turned looking for his jacket. Amelia put it in his hands the moment he was done with the towel.

"Am I late? I hope not. Amelia come give me a hug," Eve was beaming as she entered the kitchen, "Hello dear. It smells absolutely divine in here, I'm enchanted. Except for those stones."

"Seriously, Roth," Amelia added. Roth understood the point, the rocks had to go, but he loved seeing the two forge a determined coalition and be of like mind.

Eve's perfectly placed short curly hair barely reached her chin, showcasing the shape of her lean neck. She wore a sparked wired bandeau above her forehead detailed with silver and stones. A ribbon framed the length of her empire dress falling just at the knee.

"Hello darling," Roth whispered as he reached for Evelyn offering a tiny kiss.

"I love your dress, did you sew it?" Amelia asked, knowing Evelyn was keen to a new pattern and had a passion for dressmaking.

"I did, I went a bit wild buying fabrics, but at least it keeps me busy. And so what's the latest on the kids?"

"Should be here any second. Can I get you a glass of wine?" Roth asked. "Now, both of you leave the kitchen. Evelyn and Amelia will be the best hosts ever, I'll just finish the oysters and let me know when the doorbell rings, until then I am focused on the starter course."

"Okay come with me, Amelia, bring the wine. Where's Tad?"

"Hospital, they're having a baby!"

"Really! That is the most exciting thing I have heard, God bless. I can't wait to see our Lily, she has occupied so much of my time – just absolutely joyful thinking of her."

"Speak of the devil." Evelyn walked to the front door to welcome the pair "Hey you two," she called from the door, "Lily give me a kiss. Nice to see you again, Dimitri." All eyes glanced at Lily's hands, searching for a sparkle from a ring.

"Eve, you look just stunning, I love the dress and the beaded bag is to die for," Lily complimented, extending a hug to Eve.

"Amelia's inside and get this, Roth is cooking," Eve explained.

"Really, what's the rub?" Lily asked with a smile.

"Tad's out, baby on the way."

"Fabulous, I'm telling Roth to give him time off for this, he's earned it," Lily replied walking through the doorway.

"Actually, Roth seems excited, focused and can't wait

to talk to you both, get in here."

"Dad? Roth? You back here?" Lily exclaimed, searching the house.

"In the kitchen, let me pour you a glass of something. Did you see Evelyn and Amelia? They're here too. And now you, you've made my day. Hi love," Roth said welcoming them, "Dimitri, how are you son?"

"Never better. Just spent a few restful days over the bay," he replied.

Roth, Eve, and Amelia share a coy smile.

"Well you all have made this old dad remarkably happy today. A toast to you and a blessing to the new parents and child," Roth raised his glass.

"Amen," whispered Evelyn.

"Here, Here," Dimitri added.

"Have a seat everyone Kumamoto oysters to start with a light crab salad," Roth served everyone then arrived with a large rib eye roast.

"Evelyn, this is delightful, my compliments to the chef!"

"Thanks Amelia, I'll let him know," Eve smiled kicking Roth under the table.

"Dad, faith is reaching new heights, I'm resurrecting a church – I've found my way – confidently," Lily added in a hubris filled whisper.

"Inspiring, really. How can I help?"

"Well, it's a chapel really, in nature and I'm working with friends."

"Even better, tell me everything," Roth urged more details.

"No."

"Really? Why so?" Roth asked.

"You'll have to come to services."

"No problem, I would love to," Roth promised. "That's

exciting and I'm beyond curious, I can't wait to see the result of your passion and efforts."

"Well Lily," he continued. "I failed once again to have Amelia come and work for us. Sorry Evelyn, just you and me," Roth confessed.

"Dad focus," Lily retorted, "get it together - she has deep commitments. Structure it like an alliance, work together without you being an overlord. Think of it as a merger. You need to learn to share."

Laughing, Roth gave Lily the assurance her brilliant idea would be given the level of consideration it deserved and an exhaustive review from Amelia and Evelyn. Roth knew there was a point in every conversation when one should stop talking, not just to listen, but to distill, extract how and what was being suggested and to discern what was not being mentioned. He used a pause or a break as a point to reset. He could apply his usual pressure, turning lingering hope to reinforce his point. He had the uncanny ability to understand the paradox of expanding and contracting senses; the beat of an unsettled heart, the length of a full breath drawing another, the relief of jettisoned distrust and betrayal to calm earnest directives with truer intentions.

The idea came from Lily. Amelia would hear it beyond the reverberations from normal channels of communications. He had thought of the idea a few times prior, never advancing the notion for fear it would be perceived, coming from him as a power grabbing exercise to advance further domination. Eve and Amelia would socialize the prospects, Roth knew it had compelling merit and appeal.

"Ladies, I will clear the table, please join Eve on the porch. I will be in the library with Dimitri for a drink and a cigar."

"On the way, sir!" Dimitri declared.

The library was the largest room in the mansion, actually a ballroom that Roth had converted. He loved the exploration, being surrounded by different ideas and intrigue. The room was remarkably sparse, with the exception of three large chairs positioned in front of a stone fireplace, and a table that allowed for an ashtray and two glasses of fine French Armagnac. Dimitri quietly admired the accents in the bookcases and the details that reached from floor to ceiling. Wooden butterflied book holders were equally as elegant to the collection of atlases presented on a low shelf that anchored the far window. Every point of geography wasn't just a country, rather a collective of culture, faith, politics evolving for better or worse, with the aspirational pushing and pulling of society and the dreams of a community. The regal maps were colored pages adorned with lines and boundaries accurately expressing the history between nations replete with conflicts, wars, and uprisings. In the hushed opposite corner of the library sat Roth's well-read family bible, a prized heirloom with a worn leather cover.

Roth entered the room. His voice echoed as he brought wood for the fire, "If you need something to read help yourself, I'm happy to share. And if I've read it, I won't ask you for it back, no fuss. Son, I'm working on a project and it touches the East River and runs west towards Madison Square Park. Here your buildings have value, but the space above, the air rights make them even more desirable. Are you open – and I would make sure it is generous – to reasonable offers, not just for purchase, but to partnering with me to see what is possible?"

"Sure, you know I'm happy as they are, but certainly open to a conversation." Dimitri wasn't terrified to be nervous, knowing the ripple in his glass revealed a tremor requiring the support of a second hand to help bring the drink close enough to his lips where he could lean forward to take a sip.

"Glad to hear you're willing to consider it and get a sense of what is being offered. Your instincts are solid, I will send you details. You hear clearly what the wind is saying for you and Lily."

"Ring is in my pocket, I'm aiming for the next full moon."

"I have something for you." Roth walked towards a shelf with a carved wood box. He returned with an envelope with Dimitri's name on it.

"Transitions can be a challenge, just a little gift from me, I'm here to help you two."

Dimitri put the envelope in his pocket without opening it and thanked Roth for his generosity.

"Wonderful to see Evelyn," Dimitri confirmed what everyone at dinner understood. "She has a caring and loving soul."

"True," Roth acknowledged.

"And I didn't know the extent of Amelia's business?" Dimitri inquired looking for more details.

Roth leaned forward, "That's an understatement, she's a captain of industry, but because she is a woman and the dim view of many in the markets, most try to ignore her, and reach for her father. She's not to be overlooked, best in the biz in my view."

"It'll be fall soon. Lily and I will spend the end of summer dreaming of a full moon, so I hope!"

"Perfect plan," Roth inhaled his cigar, enjoying a rare sensation of control and steady family momentum.

BRUTE FORCE

FOLDING THE PAPER back into quarters, he crossed his right leg over his left as if to hug his knee and pull it closer, pointing it in the direction of Lily. Their body language encompassed a connection without a destination. Wherever and whenever they were alone, they were delightfully consumed with one another, and that was enough to feel blissfully safe and beyond comfortable. Nothing tangible defined the heartfelt notion growing between them, it was chemistry beyond their will, and the ease of a robust energy that was the underpinning of their connection. An ever-present collision of desires shared and mutually felt driving them to see, touch, and feel the depth of every cherished nano-second of their tender embrace. Dimitri's knee rose slightly above the table showcasing his cleanest pair of studio pants, the rest of his collection was covered in paint and not at a standard presentable for the local café. Thin black and white stripes oscillated inviting an arbitrary sky blue and canary yellow interlude making a dramatic appearance completing the lined pattern. He wore a natural linen shirt at work, play, and in the studio. On the street he wore a cloth waistcoat – comfortable, yet constructed enough to visit any parlor or service without a question or glance. Lily's finger traced the thin line down his knee to his tan leather loafer, clean and unmarred. A modest billfold, a clutch of matches, and a keepsake pocket watch intermittently correct, but known for being incapable of keeping time were his steady companions always close at hand.

Perplexed by the momentum of her restless fingers a thin lemon slice cruised the circle of her teacup stirred in a brew that had long since cooled. Unable to find a napkin, she licked the exotic flavor from her fingers. Dimitri's deep focus made him easy to distract. Lily would start with a coy touch that he acknowledged by covering her playful fingers, his eyes darted towards her. "All okay?" he implored with intensity. Her vague answer would follow.

"Well, I guess" Lily moved closer and blew a gentle kiss touching his ear.

"All okay?" Dimitri resumed rereading the same headline to a story he never got to finish. Lily loved his dedication to current events and the next page. She enjoyed knowing that if she distracted or interrupted him his first concern was for her safety. She paused before kissing his cheek.

"Hey, all okay?" Dimitri inquired. "Right, I get it. Let's go, it's late anyway. Let's head back."

Their morning outings usually led to afternoons without formality or structure. A slower pace, an embrace, and a sidewalk leading homeward would expand intimacy allowing them to linger and enjoy the effortlessness of these romantic journeys. Quiet side streets allowed them to relax, laugh, and duck under rain soaked awnings to hug or playfully chase one another desperate to hear each other's kaleidoscope dreams. Exciting discoveries got brighter, but not for long, they burst and fading once they crossed Canal Street.

• • •

The explosive sound thrust Lily's body crashing to the pavement. Her hands slipped and were unable to securely anchor to the sidewalk or begin lifting her body. Stunned and confused she rolled over, tasting blood in her mouth. Nearby, Dimitri's oversized fist swung in response landing with a bone-breaking blow, the man he connected with fell equally as hard to the curb below. Blood flowed from the ears of the motionless body.

"Dimitri? Dimitri? What happened?" she called out. The small crowd of onlookers was blurry. She saw they were circling the truck that had backfired and the injured man.

"Help, police! Stop that man!" one shouted pointing towards Dimitri.

He turned his double-time cadence to a hard sprint. Lily slid her body low along the wall of the building moving slowly in the opposite direction of the outcry and attention. Her clothes were wet, soiled and smelled of the gutter that she just climbed out from, and by the time the law arrived both of them were long gone. Lily covered herself in a light scarf and walked directly to Amelia's home. She struggled at the first step of the brownstone, her hand locked on the black metal railing. The steady stream of tears pouring down her cheeks was without end. She lunged, tossing her exhausted body with each step.

Across town, Dimitri sat alone in the darkness, unable to recall clearly what had happened or how he got there. The sawdust on the floor reminded him that the kitchen of the speakeasy was friendly. His third glass calmed his nerves and lowered the energy of the chaos and echoes sounding off in his mind. He rubbed his hands together wondering where Lily might have fled and knew Amelia's was the likely spot. Was there a way for this to stop? Or start a way to end or rest the blur that brought uncertainty to dissolve or dissipate or vacate it entirely? Why was he still fighting constantly?

Dimitri ducked into the Center for Servicemen, finding his old cot in the rear corner of the open room on the second floor. It smelled familiar and made him thankful, lucky to have an extended family. He imagined writing a note to Amelia. He stood up and scanned the room looking for a note card and a pencil only to pause, having forgotten why he was standing back at his cot. He was fast asleep. Routine found Dimitri up early, making his bed and quickly shaving. The headline that morning read of the "senseless assault on a local physician," and that a manhunt that was underway. Reading this he understood what happened and remembered running from the scene, but not the loud explosion that triggered his punch. He took refuge in the back row of the daily prayer service held on the first floor. He remembered the words! He was especially impressed recalling the timing of the service. His participation in the shared chorus was a milestone and meaningful victory. It didn't, however, remove the layers of doubt and cycle of questions keeping the faint notion of mental dexterity and control at a distance. His sore hands reminded him to keep moving. The jovial elevated voices got louder as he headed out of services. At the end of the aisle he was greeted by a meandering collection of senior staff. Their presence meant something larger was underway. Stepping into the hallway, Dimitri snapped to attention. Col. Chamberlain approached the saluting soldiers.

"You look hearty, we could use your help," Col. Chamberlain announced handing Dimitri a wanted flyer.

"Sir, yes Sir, ready to help. I'll get moving right away," Dimitri saluted command and made a swift exit.

The Colonel offered his regiment in support of the law enforcement effort to track down the violent assailant. His presence amplified the mission. The community's rally to bring urgency and attention to public safety wasn't a surprise. The number of those in attendance that evening had surpassed all expectations. The Colonel assured the public that their coordinated search would find success.

Amelia was a good listener, unfazed and stoic as Lily unpacked the events and tried not to see the newspaper in front of them.

"I'm just sure if he is okay now he will go to the cottage, right? He can't go home! Should he turn himself in?" she pondered.

"Just give it time, he needs to find his head again and he'll find us I'm sure of it." Amelia was a great cheerleader for Lily.

A merciless headache and her scratched lip were her only physical reminders of what had happened. This rage surely was familiar, wasn't it? Why did it come with such abundance and bedlam determined on upending the serenity of her otherwise calm existence? This violence was self-propelled trauma, unfocused and raw, but thankfully, she surmised, it was not directed at her.

"All okay, honey?" she whispered under her breath, wishing her prayer for Dimitri received a larger audience. She was pre-occupied with a painful uncertainty that loitered on every thought and tortured every muscle. How deep did this wound go?

URGENT BLISS

W AIT, THAT'S MY boat," Stephen turned from the conversation leaping over the tall sea grass that lined the dune, sprinting into the ocean. Amelia and Lily were not completely alarmed, at least not yet. Dimitri had never seen Stephen race to the beach and then into the water. Stephen's mate was trying to keep the boat close to shore; the overloaded engine struggled forward and then in reverse, making low sputtering sounds. He knew trouble was near.

"They're at the bay"

"What? Who?" Stephen reached up and hoisted himself on the bow. He listened as Andre, his trusted first mate, explained a team of agents had two boats and were planning to cross the bay as soon as the fog lifted over the bay.

He spoke an elegant dialect, a Caribbean language with French roots perhaps, Lily thought. His skin was a deep rosewood ebony color and the shadow that fell near his body was surprisingly bright like shiny copper. He had large eyes and a smile that radiated energy. He was magnificent and at ease, clearly a steady presence in a storm.

"Have Sister Maureen flag the inlet, and slowly move across the bay, stick close to shore and then duck inside silver point and I'll find you when it quiets down."

Andre took his hand and helped lower him back into

the waves. Stephen raised his knees over the crashing waves racing up the beach.

"What language was that?" Amelia asked.

"All of them, he's quite the expert and a patient tutor."

"What's the temperature?" Dimitri asked.

"Ladies, get ready to go, grab what you need." Stephen looked rather serious.

"How bad is it?" Dimitri asked again.

"Not good, hard to be sure."

"You or me?" Dimitri inquired with a chuckle, as if there was a discernible distinction. The pair saw a large red sheet cover Maureen's window across the thin channel.

"What are you thinking? I know this look." Dimitri inquired. He knew Stephen had a plan.

"Piero's got family south of us, quick and quiet," Stephen directed.

Stephen had a cousin in law enforcement who knew a lot of things. The agents thought the high ground was a threat, and likely felt anyone on the island wouldn't last long among the bugs, snakes, or more so the sun overhead. Better to wait and have the isolated runners come to us, typical, Stephen thought to himself.

"Let's get everyone moving now," Dimitri ordered.

"Andre says they're waiting for the fog, they're concerned about the hills being an advantage to anyone on the island, follow me."

"Lily was that your mate, or mine? Amelia teased.

"I'd never call him that, he's twice the sailor I am, just don't tell him. We grew up on different ships together; same dock, same storms, some were big weather events. Interestingly, I've never seen him on land, ever," Stephen explained to her.

"Holy Mother, please have Andre's smile shine again on Lily and me," Amelia continued.

"No joke, he's a believer. I'd say he's a bit of a mystic and kinda brilliant, but that's blasphemy. They say he prayed for wind once and it came. I wouldn't have believed it, if I hadn't seen it with my own two eyes. You should have seen the reverence that flowed through him," Stephen explained.

The foursome made the dash to the cove in a short minute; Lily wasn't even out of breath or lacking in any degree of curiosity. "Why run, did you do something?" she inquired.

"I know you have questions, I will answer all of them, just give me a second, I need to get this right. Watch your step, this way," Stephen directed.

Stephen ushered the group into a narrow cavern entrance set in a small patch of trees at the foot of the hill to the meadow.

"Watch your step and hold the rope on the wall," he assured the group.

"Dimitri?"

Her eyes expressed an inkling of concern and cast thoughts of disappointment.

"Lily, are you the kind of woman who likes to try new things?" Dimitri jested.

"Seriously Lily, when have you ever had this kind of adventure?" Amelia cracked.

A curved metal staircase directed them to the bottom of a rocky damp storage area.

"Watch your eyes, I'll get the lights."

Stephen reached out, turning a timing knob that sparked and buzzed, illuminating the cave they had unknowingly entered. The mouth of the cavern met the water, serving as a natural dock, the rear of the cave was racked with inventory.

"Wow Stephen you've been busy," Dimitri noted the interior of the cave was built out with shelves, cases of product, electrical fixtures and fans.

"We've had success using this place for storage, and sanctuary," he beamed proudly. "Watch out, I'm going to lower her down." Stephen pointed to a freshly stained and painted long deck launch.

"She's stunning," Dimitri noted looking at the large boat suspended from the ceiling overhead.

"Hey," Lily retorted with false playful jealousy.

"Let me get her started, and climb aboard and hold on."

"You think he went fast in the bay, get ready"

Lily and Amelia shared a glance of mutual concern amid the urging of betrayal from the worry of probing questions that began to swirl between them.

"Anyone have time for a quick question?" Lily smiled.

"Indulge me, I won't waste your time and I'll give you a complete answer as soon as we shove off."

Stephen hastily explained the plumbing and electric at the cottage was the proper cover for installing the lift.

"Will agents ever find any of your inventory?" Dimitri inquired.

"The cave acts as a natural trap, if you don't know the tides your boat is destroyed or at best your team is delayed, it's perfect. The cave is a transfer point, not a warehouse. Prefect for our runners to find shelter, and disappear. The law out here doesn't really reach beyond the bay, who'd understand any of it. Jump in!" Stephen ordered.

The motor reverberated throughout the enormous cave as engine fumes coated their lips. Dimitri placed a tank of fuel and a short barrel of freshwater in the rear of the boat.

"I'm scared," Amelia confessed.

"Good," shouted Dimitri, "anyone outpacing the law should be, just hang on."

Dimitri reminded Lily of their arrival during the first trip to the cottage.

"Remember what I told you, he's not stopping this thing."

"Gotta time it right, hhhhere we goooo...," Stephen said. The outgoing waves ushered the motorboat toward the narrow opening. The nose aimed lower into the water as they fell to the bottom of a wave, Dimitri's head was inches from the roof of the entrance.

"C'mon Mary Anne," Stephen exhaled.

For an anxious instant, the boat paused, then vaulted skyward as he pulled the throttle forward sending the passengers tumbling backwards across their chairs. Three large rocks guarded the entrance, saluting Captain Stephen's successful passing through the almost invisible entrance to the cave. He urged the party to shield themselves from the stinging, salt and splash of the surf. Stephen knew the fog lingered in the bay until the evening shift in atmosphere blew the pressure and humidity beyond the island. Stephen hugged the coast hoping to insulate the sound of their escape until he was long past the island. Lunging and lurching, Stephen held himself in place as the launch skipped, and crashed over waves. He turned to Dimitri, all smiles.

"Not so many craft out this way, but when we get there we'll look like late cruisers," Stephen explained the last of his plans.

"Can I drive her?" Dimitri begged.

"No," objected Lily, her head on Dimitri's lap, "We're resting." Amelia was lying nearby.

"Come on, you own a piece of her, not on paper, but there are really deep connections" Stephen offered with a large grin.

"Straight out till you see a marker, head due west, take it slow when you reach the point."

"Are there mines out here?" Dimitri moved the wheel, feeling the call and the answer of the waves.

"What?! Lily shouted rubbing her eyes, "what are you two up to?"

Stephen remained calm, "If you see one let me know. You may see a channel marker, they can also be a bit tricky, but if you do, don't fret. I know the way."

Dimitri's eyes took a moment to adjust to the vast ocean before him. Minute after minute, he stared at the horizon. The pitch of the motor and the skipping of the boat over the crashing waves limited conversation, too windswept for pleasantries or shouted words. A smile and reassuring eyes said enough. Hiding under Stephen's jacket, Lily whispered a sincere apology to Amelia for the drama and unexpected turn of events.

"Nonsense. I love his strength and that he is so protective of you and focused on you – besides this is exciting!" Amelia confessed with emotion.

"Is that land?" Dimitri asked.

"Land aye," Stephen replied. He started moving around the boat, exchanging attentive glances with the passengers. Stephen placed baskets and fishing items around the cabin.

"Take a wide tack, smoothly into the channel, no wake on the action side of the wharf," Stephen commanded. The slow speed was reassuring and a comfort compared to the dash across the open ocean. They were safe, protected by distance and the length of the endless shore. As they entered the channel Stephen noticed an unusual presence and directed Dimitri to dock close by on the port side. The group quickly stepped onto the dock as the launch was covered with cargo and tarps, becoming barely recognizable.

The new law enforcement concern focused on Dimitri required smart, urgent, and efficient decisions. Stephen inquired with his colleagues on the dock, former Navy seamen if there was any official movement on the dock. In the hour it took for the new boat to clear the protocols for docking at the wharf, Stephen was ready to move further inland. Cheng's awaited. He didn't return lightly, and it was time to close the chapter on the nerves and impairment of his good name, self-maligned by hubris and the humanity he displayed there. It would take strength to arrive and not keep one's eyes fixed burning a hole deep into the ground.

Stephen had friends and Piero arrived with a wide armed hug and a kiss. He thanked him for his swift distraction and instant protection for him and his travel mates. Piero owned the dock and whatever duty he demanded, was well worth it. If he intonated something was not possible, to Stephen, it was not. Others were unwittingly being upsold in a losing negotiation. Piero offered his own boat. Stephen smiled knowing its passage would be completely unchallenged. Piero extended only a select few runners safe passage, a gatekeeper to the deeper ocean. Piero demanded and expected discretion on his dock. With a paternal quality he embraced, "My young Captain." The end of day on the dock included a standing invitation to Stephen to a private dining room. They were seldom planned, and felt like a family reunion. Piero's guests were showered with hospitality, all indulging in food, wine, and fine coffee. Menu offerings included unique items fresh from the wharf, candid language, and Piero offering a duet, his eyes working to the cadence of his imaginary partner. Only Piero could hear the flute, the allure of the longing string section. His eyes engaged with the group, his arms creating a swirl of full orchestration. A second acknowledgement to his unpresent partner, his arms lifted the aria grander and higher to a complete applause. The encore was equally as grand; a deep-bellied Faustian roll of laughter, Stephen had seen it on many occasions amidst flowing wine while standing on chairs or the highest stool. The many bottles always welcome stories of victories of Italian alpine soldiers battling in the northern Alps. Bold offensives that outshone passive neutrality, Piero felt pride in the victory of the mighty Alpini, and a strong alliance with those at supper.

No one on the dock spoke Italian with any degree of success, Piero's understanding and urgency rang out with a universal intensity. He was the lone tenor, a grand voice in constant motion, Stephen was unfazed by the direction and the result. Piero caught many off guard, Stephen knew the landscape and would privately muse, wondering how someone working on the dock was so tailored and polished. Who made these suits, shirts, and hats? The details on his boat were another elegant accessory. Stephen knew Piero's trust had no limit, and that he enjoyed his complete confidence. He also knew who was in charge around the inner waterway, and to not bring your troubles or your embarrassing behavior to his second floor parlor. As they were about to shove off, Piero asked Stephen in a whisper to meet his cousin at his seasonal tent by the Great Auditorium. "Leave the boat with him, he'll have clear instructions and a way to keep your group protected and together," Piero said.

"Grazie mille," Stephen offered under his breath as he released Piero's hand, knowing an elevated voice would likely offend. The boat shoved off, Stephen knowing the next part of the journey would only take an hour.

Both sides of the inlet gently moved together, one side towards the other. A flotilla of boats bound together, full of purpose and good cheer. A long, overstretched, rope adorned with ribbons and flags was held hand in hand. Anticipation grew across the waterway. A communal connection joining land and sea was symbolic of the bond of the arriving bride and groom. Their approach, one from each side, merged dreams of a beach side family with an ocean side family. The Reverend found the middle boat arriving on his own launch; he would speak of ancestry and a bright future, full of promise. Lanterns and lights that were strung overhead were illuminated, as were the candles that graced the tables across the wharf. The wind was calm.

The music, prayers and words kept the inlet focused ensuring a discreet and unremarkable exit for the foursome. Waving among the wedding party with blessings and approval, Piero found his position among the other well-wishers on the wharf. He could only hope to offer a topping aria to serenade the couple as they would later dance, he'd sing from his heart and offer a raise to the young couple from his coffers. Everyone paused, amid the love struck connection that joined the pair in union.

The slow, ever expanding ripple grew wider and wider as the soft splash of a skipping stone quietly came to rest. A stillness lingered in the inlet, as solemn vows were whispered across the water.

BLUE MOON

STEPHEN CUT THE engine. He would row to the dock with just a single oar to be discreet and make the group aware that quiet will keep trouble focused on other places. The women all knew Stephen more than he would like to admit. Churning sin shame and fear sweat accompanied quiet soul searching with his first step back on to Doc. Pinco Cheng's landing. He focused on securing the lines as Lily and Amelia shared a puzzled look. His arrival is greeted by calls from the open nearby windows.

"I miss you, now come see me. Stop right there Stephen honey, and have a sip of whisky with me. I know you know the taste of my lips are sweeter with you near."

"It's not what you think, I'm here twice a week for fuel, food, smokes, on deliveries, sometimes they invite me in for a drink," Stephen tried to explain.

"Never explain yourself," Dimitri added with a grin, "you'll just bring more questions. How do you break up that much love?"

Stephen wondered if Doc. Cheng's women could still remember his unique flavor and the taste of his skin. He looked away touching the tip of his nose with a scratch, remembering the lingering hint of perfume that held allure. His shy demeanor was amplified by the shame. He stared hard at his feet and was grateful Amelia couldn't hear the pounding emotions swirling in his head. Stephen describes Doc. Cheng's "family" as loving and loyal; when you hug them you get fragrance and a hint of sweat from a very active lifestyle. There was unity among them amid needless violence and ruthless men. Their dwelling was an aspirational English speaking enterprise, but their work was a global expression hosting many cultures, languages, and techniques.

Most found Doc. Cheng's by following the cooking smells, which hovered low along the water at mealtime. Passionate culinary notes that find your body the way the melody of a well-played string instrument gently strokes the ear in a soothing and inviting way, urgently pulling you closer.

Doc. Cheng's compound was not accessible by road, he focused on supplying and feeding all who travel by water from Pleasure Bay through Husky Creek. Three two story homes offered lodging and an active pantry that supported the outdoor kitchen on the dock. Doc. Pinco Cheng's arrival was a welcome embrace. He wore a long indigo robe with gold trim that was vibrant and flowing.

He greeted Stephen with a hug asking, "How's the molar?"

"Does it have to come out?" Stephen worried.

"You know, they all may at their right moment. Only the tooth knows, let me see what it's telling us."

Doc. Cheng was the closest thing to a dentist for much of the region's seafaring community. Looking through his glasses he stared deeply into Stephen's mouth.

"Sea bugs," Dimitri teased, "what's in there?"

"No bugs in here, sea lice is no laughing matter by the way. It appears the haworth bend is broken, let me know if it starts to cause you pain. Take these." Doc. Cheng offered

Stephen sticks of cloves to help soothe the tooth.

Doc. Cheng directed the group to the main house and instructed Stephen to light a fire. "Ladies, let me offer you a nightcap? I have a wide selection," he offered.

Lily and Amelia made their way into the bedroom to inventory the bedding and towels and were pleasantly relieved to find two well-made beds. Doc. Cheng uncorked a bottle.

"Who will come tomorrow afternoon?"

"The usual look-in," Stephen explained. "Keep your stock away from the water. These guys with the shoes they're wearing won't even leave the boat. Feed'em, gas'em, and tell'em we talked about our shipping friends beyond town."

"You know I don't allow these sorts of problems on my dock."

"Doc. Cheng, it's out of my hands. It's just tonight, and we'll be up and out early," Stephen promised.

With a nod, Doc. Cheng returned to the cooking fire on the dock, the ambers burned yellow as he prepared a fish stew with chopped noodles. The constant rhythm from the slap of his tools against the wok intensified. With a mesmerizing swish the contents were placed into a large shallow bowl announcing to the group that dinner service had commenced. Seating on the dock was family-style, and rustic. Rough wooden benches framed an unrefined table. The fire from the stove lit the outdoor kitchen, a single bulb hung overhead. Anchoring the opposite end of the table, Dimitri sat heavy-hearted. His burdensome gaze focused on a single unlit cigarette he rolled between his finger and his thumb. Stephen's arrival was celebrated as he hoisted a pail of beer from the cold water, placing it in the center of the table. He had complete confidence the eclectic menu would surprise and exceed the expectations of all of Doc. Cheng's guests. The combination of salt, soy, and garlic added to the magic of Doc. Cheng's cooking. Lily and Amelia were reluctant at first, but the first taste had them.

PILGRIMS' PATH

THEY ARRIVED JOSTLED and disheveled with windblown hair and ears full of sand. Romero, Piero's cousin welcomed them with commitment and an assurance of safe passage.

"Piero, of course, told me nothing beyond your safety and travel was of the utmost importance and to handle it with urgency and discretion. You have no worries here. However, if your schedule allows, especially if you're praying on something or praying for others, you're in the right place. Some folks visit and end up staying the whole season. All are welcome, it's sort of come as you are. It's really lovely to experience."

Romero's arms gestured toward the majestic sanctuary that towered over the beach community.

"Faith runs deep here, you can feel pastoral divinity in the air that extends beyond the walls. Please consider staying a while, I insist, you must stay with us."

Ironically, Romero never attended Sunday service in-person, but he prayed everyday, rejoicing in the choir and the sermons from afar. His sweat and oversight helped build The Great Auditorium. From foundation to expansion he knew every bolt, system, hook, and book in the sanctuary. Job security came in knowing every nail, switch and crack in need of attention. He was artful in building harmony and managing conflict in the community. His uniform was a smile, and summertime denim. He was respected by all who defined his work circle and family. He did have to endure the occasional down looker who never admitted to their own vices. Romero understood the value of keeping one's hands moving. Worry was faithless. He found a melody in dividing jobs and projects to grow participation. Larger action moving in lockstep was the unifying goal. Strength and upholding every aspect of each other's lives and work came easy. He was a prime example of the dignified approach to the ethic of collaborative work. Anyone who wanted to work with Romero was regarded as family - an expressed dedication to those who labored. He took great pride in his work and the recognition that the collective of those who labored built this great nation and protected other nations around the globe. Romero gravitated toward less understood outcomes, expanding faithful emotions with a steadfast commitment towards justice.

He often divided simple tasks among two or more workers. The idea went beyond a wage for a day, to build relationships, partnerships and new alliances that he would incubate becoming resilient, trusted, which would extend generationally.

Surrounding the Church were rows of small tents open to a plaza that extended to the shore. The encampment was more precisely a bungalow topped with a vibrant awning flowing from a center peak. Blue and white scalloped edge fabric draped the sides and face of the porch creating a private cabana space. The shadowed overhang appeared almost black in contrast to the bright midday sun. The rear of the homes was a structure for shelter, but most of the sleeping took place in the open center. Wind, song, and faith defined the encampment. Children ran the length of the walk that stretched from the ocean waves to the Church door. Their gaggle of laughter was at a volume slightly higher than was generally permissible. Three nearby chairs on the edge of the shade defined a well-used outdoor reading room. Each day ended with quiet reflection, centered minds present and richly optimistic.

Romero was there even when he didn't need to be, and he was always on the move. If he had no projects underway, he cleaned, swept or had a hose in tow. He took great pride in making certain all pathways and gardens surrounding the Church were fastidiously maintained. His consistent presence brought a sense of order and control that was reassuring to the community. He took great joy being surrounded by his entire family. All cooked, shopped, cleaned and prepared, it wasn't work, but a movement with its own unique cadence, a melodic orchestration that heightened their faith and unity. Lily was enchanted by the small garden full of lush herbs and spices, her nose found the aroma of basil leading to a smile. She was intent on helping prep the supper that was already in formation.

"Can we sleep outside?" Lily inquired with exuberance.

"You won't be alone," Romero's eyes expanded as his oversized face blushed, "I mean it can be communal. Ah, that didn't sound right either. Lot of people do it – forget it, sleep where you want."

"Hear that Dimitri, anywhere." Her smile was inviting.

"Come sit, everybody we can start with salad and bread. Romero usually has much to say, so Dimitri if you would, a blessing for the table." Romero's wife Natalie directed all of her guests to their seats. Dimitri offered open hands and bowed his head in a prayer. He added a bit silently after the word Amen. He prayed for the recovery of the gentleman he unintentionally assaulted and that the embarrassment of being a burden to others, those he loved, would end. Dimitri was quiet through the salad course Natalie prepared with great care. Fresh herbs and cheeses were the highlights, and Dimitri was reminded that the company you dine with really does elevate the experience. Romero asked questions throughout the meal. The collection of responses led to big tales; journeymen laughter followed as Natalie would translate his tall-tales into their unvarnished and essential truthfulness. Romero rolled his eyes as the laughter continued, long passed the pour of the last bottle of wine.

The oversized sofa covered in pillows and a weighty blanket was all the invitation Dimitri needed. He quietly thanked Natalie for the extravagant supper and intended to fall fast asleep. He realized that he was masking his worry to not cause concern for Lily. The calming wind coming off the ocean was perfect for introspection, and time to process his behavior. He felt the weight of justice tighten his body. His soul was always guided by doing what was right with a deep commitment to what was honorable, so why was this different? He thought he could turn himself in, but that thought was short-lived, distracted by the cuddle of Lily who decided it was time to pull the blanket they were sharing to her chin and close her eyes. Dimitri stayed awake most of the night. The hushed tent was the perfect trap to elevate his rolling feelings of guilt and his disorganized thoughts. Fading in and out of consciousness, it was a tap on his shoulder from Romero who whispered an invitation to a cup of hot coffee putting an end to his anguish and reminding Dimitri that it was a new day full of possibilities.

The strategy to move everyone swiftly and discreetly beyond the Church required Romero's mastery of local logistics. A weekend excursion to the marina was the cover for their early morning movements. Romero planned to divide the foursome into two subsets as to be less conspicuous for any who took note. Romero, being up and about early, didn't garner a second glance; his morning routine hadn't changed in years. Once they reached the boardwalk, a brief stroll to a waiting delivery van drove them to the next leg of their journey. Marina life met dawn with soft words and light footsteps. The cove of the Shark River was protected and gave the group the unnoticed exit they needed.

"You can take it from here?" Romero invited Stephen to captain the small tender that would taxi the young couples.

"I will, thank you," Stephen replied, starting the small motor.

Dimitri saw what was coming next just beyond the jetty. The artful lines and the flawless details were breathtaking.

"Dimitri, Piero wants you to head out on this one, she's part of the fleet, a really elegant addition. Tell no one where you are heading. The charts in the wheelhouse are a loving suggestion from us. My guys stocked it full, you're ready to roll, don't miss the tide."

Dimitri and Lily hugged their friends and thanked Romero for his hospitality.

"Next time, we'll join you for the season. Thanks for everything my friend. Till next time." Dimitri climbed the small ladder hanging from the stern of the boat. He turned and reached for Lily's arm.

"Now, Stephen I have some instructions for you from Piero. It involves a conversation with a captain who works closely with him. Word is that he may be retiring soon.

He's anchored just beyond the inlet. He will protect you and Amelia. Piero would like you to present a mutually suitable arrangement to him, you'll understand once you're on board."

After a few minutes, Stephen understood Piero's intentions. The slight trace of an outline of a ship started to reveal itself, slowly emerging from a magical segue point where the sea and sky merge. The distant horizon was a brushstroke blurred, a blend of fog and soft blue haze. The vessel was a small freighter with the build of a tugboat. It wore a color without distinction, Stephen had seen it a million times, but it didn't have a precise name. It was mostly red, sometimes orange accented by rust. It had two cargo areas, two cranes, and waterside docks on both sides of the ship. It would be a floating storage facility positioned far off shore.

"Head to a place north of here called Lunenburg," Romero relayed.

Stephen understood that this was now a significant expansion to store Canadian Whiskey and products from Ireland and the United Kingdom.

"I'll check in once we're in position. And thank you, and Piero as well," Stephen said. Without another word, Romero motored back toward the Marina, wishing them well, he and Natalie would spend the evening chatting about the lovely young couples, he would keep them in his prayers.

Stephen and Amelia reached for the metal platform and clumsily climbed aboard. A man stood waiting for them.

"Welcome aboard, I'm Nigel, the Ex. O., they told me it was just one man, but this is not the first time we've had a stowaway. Do me a favor and lay low until I can explain you being on board to the boss," he said. "You'll both stay in my cabin, and meals will be delivered. Once you get settled Stephen, we'll go and see the Captain. And if it's not too much of a bother, ma'am, I'd ask you to wear this cap and denim jacket if you venture out," Nigel suggested removing his jacket and cover.

Stephen always learned the new map of a boat by counting steps and stairs. He now knew that five steps carried him to the main stairs, six steps twice got him to their tiny berth, and the last two steps past the bulkhead led to the Wheelhouse.

"Thanks Nigel, this should be perfect."

Nigel turned closing the narrow door. The space in the room was just big enough for two people to stand and small enough for little else except climbing into the sleeping berth. A small bathroom was adjacent.

"Well this is cozy, and since food is delivered and you can't wander about, I think you should make yourself comfortable," Stephen said smiling.

Stephen was superstitious about romance. He knew the difference between like and love was only about ninety degrees. He faced Amelia smiling as she stood south of him. He couldn't have felt more jubilant as he held her hands. Facing a partner in the east was an amorous delay, a meaningful but certain damnation of a lasting, yet heartfelt acquaintanceship. As their cheeks tenderly made contact Amelia whispered, "Exhaustion?"

"Rejuvenation," Stephen replied.

"Why do it?" she asked.

"How can you stop?" he questioned.

"When would you know?" Amelia took the game further.

"Who would I tell?" Stephen admitted how few others he had to confide in, to the degree he knew he could with Amelia.

Their game of dancing questions softly spoken found Amelia sitting on his lap, playfully exchanging sweet and salty kisses.

The tap on the door greeted the pair with fresh rolls and hot coffee.

"Captain will be ready for you in one hour, and I mentioned your travel companion to him, he just smiled," Nigel shared.

"Terrific, thanks for everything."

Stephen soon walked up the two steps toward the bridge, pausing as he entered to recognize the Captain, out of the utmost respect for command.

"Captain, Sir, thank you for giving me a moment of your time and for your hospitality and for that of your crew."

"At ease son, what is on your mind?"

"Piero thought you and I should have a conversation about some of the importing and exporting that is reaching his wharf. He would like you and I to form a mutually beneficial alliance. Leveraging my network of distribution and your assets for offshore storage and movement."

The Captain paused to reflect on the suggestion. A blunt reality meeting the homegrown integrity of a self-made man. The market would expand with him, or pass him by. Collaboration had appeal and contrasted with the rigid solitude of his current approach.

"Well he does have solid instincts about our work, let me consider your proposal today and we can discuss details in the mess for supper, and bring your guest. Welcome aboard."

"Thank you sir," Stephen said before leaving.

"Plot a course towards Lunenburg," the Captain ordered.

GOD'S GRACE

"**I**SN'T THIS JUST glorious?" Lily swirled around the tiny cabin. Warm sunbeams refracted through four narrow windows detailing both sides of the boat and lit the rich mahogany aglow. Lily hoisted her dress swiftly over her head, her skin tan and radiant.

"Dimitri? Are you alright?"

Motionless and silent Dimitri continued to press his fist firmly against the small shelf next to his bunk, a small bible rested near his pillow.

"I'm gonna make us a sandwich for later, share some grapes? Dimitri?" Lily continued.

Silence cursed the cabin. The vessel was halfway moored in unexpressed denial and swallowed words.

"Damn KDD," he mumbled, "I have a desperate feeling I left a good man in the battle."

Lily moved closer. "You didn't mean to hurt anyone, the center is helping you and many others. You've made incredible progress."

"I prayed for his recovery all night," Dimitri said. "It doesn't matter, I'll get found out – the truth always shines. That's how it is, but this is going to impact Amelia, the center, and stain the solid reputation of a lot of the men. I'm going to write Col. Chamberlain a letter, a real letter. I've got to tell the truth. This will give Stephen the time he needs, and for me I know what awaits. I should be accountable, and leave the rest up to God's good grace."

"It's not your fault, but I admire your integrity," Lily said. She grabbed a small towel to wipe the sweat from his forehead. "I'll let Amelia know too, she's pretty good at working things through. We can escape this, but could you live with yourself if we did? It's also important to have this be a larger conversation about how the men are doing now that some time has passed."

"Don't tell Roth, wait, maybe we should. Lily, I am so sorry."

"Tell him, he'll try and help"

"I gotta fix this, fight to make it right."

"I'll help."

Dimitri's frustration started to ease, a deep sigh announcing his liberation from the paralyzing guilt that weighed heavily on him. With a plan and Lily's support, he was confident he could confront his challenges in a direct and honest way. His confession, regardless of consequence, genuinely elevated his authenticity as he continued to strive to create a larger presence in the eye of honor.

"Alright, let's get underway!"

WESTERN STORMS

LIKELY THE FIRST polished cobbler crafted leather sole to touch the island in years. Andre got a good look. The shoes had a perfect mirrored shine. They weren't law enforcement this was private. Their jackets were removed in the sun revealing their firepower and showcasing their misplaced attire. Only two crossed the bay, a third heading in the direction of Piero's wharf. The search of the island was a quick look through; they didn't hope to stay for an extended visit.

A large oversized envelope was left on the table near the kitchen in the cottage. The lead and his partner were back on the boat returning across the bay, each working a handkerchief trying to remove sand from their toes.

BEST WISHES

THE COLLAPSE OF the crescent moon haunted the emergence of a wobbly waxing gibbous, that later invited, then hid from, the first of two full moons to which Dimitri was utterly and completely oblivious. Routine business kept G.G. on watch overnight, pacing, never straying or moving far from the cottage. Roth's lonely envelope sat unseen and unopened for a period extending more than a couple of months, a first for any of his offers.

Roth displayed design and form in all of his projects. He reviewed the look, shape, and feel as a student of art history always reexamining, searching for the essence of an idea, and confident enough in his vision to pause and ask why. He had a remarkable innate instinct to see more than a building, absorbing every dimension and possibility, understanding its harmony, interaction and impact.

The next part of his approach was an assessment of its viability and discovering what was possible across a range of questions. A combination of transactional, but important items necessary to address early, to understand the full vitality of the landscape. His finance training directed him to look at the amount of materials, weight and the movement of the same, number of work crews, and time. Always time, every time. Only when he had a complete sense of the effort and the equation that was in balance, he acted divisively. His passion usually made him first to capitalize on an idea. His time creating and investing in the preparation for a project could take years. It was not uncommon for him to have his team visit sites he was not interested in to distract his rivals. The time-consuming nature of his research added value, his proposals needed to be protected and communicated with urgency, and only through trusted hands. To ensure security and discretion Roth hired agents who followed his request to hand-deliver the proposal directly to Dimitri's cottage.

Son-
Property in town is the keystone to a larger deal. Think height, span, the scale is quite significant. Please read the terms and note the down payment ensuring consideration and that the new venture is underway. It will prove to be substantial; look forward to your review, input and partnership. The documents have exhaustive instructions on where to sign and next steps. Hope to see you both soon.

Best Wishes,
-Roth

Evelyn's rapport with Amelia remained uninterrupted. The exciting possibility of joining forces in the future wouldn't require a new introduction. The pair wrote almost daily and had become well established allies who collaborated on a number of community and service-minded ventures unrelated to business. Each gracefully possessed a level-winged approach toward their work, complimented by a patient temperament ensuring they could out-command any would be takers.

My Dearest Amelia,

All pieces in motion.
All sandy acres surrounding the bay will be protected lands.
The birds will love it.
The lovebirds will enjoy the island and especially your gift extending the tract westward.
The new venture is underway.

Clear Skies,
-Eve

BIG DREAMS

THE CAPTAIN FINISHED his last bit of seared cod and gently placed his utensils on the plate.

"Son, I understand what makes sense and Piero is right to find alignment among like minded sailors. We're not pirates. So, the idea of joining forces I'm wide open to talking about further."

"Great, I can hear Piero singing already," Stephen said.

"How true, we need to consider the wide reach and expansion. I suggest working two shifts six days a week. You can come and go as you please, I'll be on site and can handle management here. The crews will need transport and we need a base for on-land operations. Ideally, an area that is not heavily traveled, some place remote so as to not draw attention. It maybe worth considering, since the Sound is friendly to Rhode Island building a stronger trail up the Connecticut River, it would shore up the region," The Captain explained.

"O' I think I have an idea…," Amelia attempted.

"Not now honey," Stephen said.

"But it's perfect"

"Honey, let the Captain finish."

"But the cottage is in the center of a newly established nature sanctuary the road is only open to land owners and there aren't that many. Sister Maureen's point is perfect for a headquarters."

"You know what? Captain, she's right! It's perfect. And Maureen's got a hardworking team, ready to go."

"Very good, makes no difference to me. I won't be touching land. That's for you and Piero to explore further."

"It's perfect, close to Piero, but far enough to be under the radar."

"So moving forward, we'll become operational and as a matter of timeline, I will likely make a transition in the years ahead. My share of the venture and the ship can be looked at then, I intend to continue to captain in retirement. Someplace warm, I won't be strolling on the sand."

"It will be properly valued with full compensation. Piero and I are committed to the short and long-term outlook."

The Captain extended his hand to Stephen.

"Well, I want to thank you both for joining me tonight, it's rare we have such lovely guests in the Captain's Mess. Please stay as long as you like, good night."

"Good night, sir."

The Captain turned and exited with his usual efficiency.

"Thanks honey, that went well. He's the sort who will ensure success. That was a great suggestion, I hadn't heard of the nature sanctuary."

"Lot of us are working behind the scenes to ensure it gets done, just don't tell Dimitri or Lily. It's part of a larger surprise. My business mind is thinking it would make sense to purchase some of the neighboring properties by Maureen's place. If your team is the only customer of supplies, gas, and food, we should create some sort of company store and manage it. It would be a well-capitalized store," she assured him.

Stephen realized Piero's plan would by any estimation make him rich. He sat quietly.

"Listen, Maureen and her team are strong, we need to expand their duties, all of them. They're going to make a lot of money. We'll do it together, that's how it will be a success."

His focus shifted. Stephen started calculating the resources to create a very remote raw bar away from regular channels, reachable only by boat. He imagined a discreet place to disappear to during celebrations.

"Have you ever spent New Year's at sea? Ever see the Northern Lights? He asked.

"I am currently not committed, but I'm willing to consider a serious invitation," she replied, smiling.

STAR HAVEN

I N THE NINE hours that passed, Dimitri was getting the needed expertise on the narrow channel that guided them through the inlet. The open bay in front of them, he reviewed and rechecked the depth of every point on the navigational chart. Piero's cousin suggested entering via the deep passage at Bonds near Sea Haven, a seascape only known to a few claimers and sun bathers of a certain pedigree, just beyond Barnegat Light to a place that had never been lived in.

"I'm keeping this boat. Calling her Mary Agnes, will Piero and Stephen understand?"

Dimitri was lost in the currents of an expanding daydream, wondering if he could sail all the way through tomorrow's sunrise, all the way to Ballycurrane and back again.

He radiated purpose and boundless energy. A tiny token of motion, a compliment to the expanse of the endless water and clear skies. Dimitri navigated close to shore past Spray Beach, he could almost see a trace of Sandy Hook behind him and Brigantine beyond. A hard rolling breeze filled both sails igniting a new race. The boat began to heel to one side Dimitri made a slight steering adjustment that seemed to lift the vessel to a space just above the water. She cut through the breaks, gliding urgently atop the waves.

"Yup, I'm keeping her," Dimitri declared. "I hope Piero and Stephen can work this out!"

"Yes please!" Lily echoed.

Looking skyward, Lily counted fourteen small winkles in the sail, she turned her head away from the forceful wind using a sheer scarf to shield her eyes from the crisp light. Dimitri moved in every direction at the same time, he worked the ropes, trimmed the sails, while still able to steer the boat. He was entertained by a sparkly school of fast agile runners, splashing and urgently keeping pace with the bow. The vessel's direction shifted in an instant as the boom tracked from one side of the boat to the other. Sound met velocity as the enormous sail snapped to attention with an ear-shattering clap. Dimitri remembered the gentle flowing movements of the white sheets that hung on the line to dry, a far-off memory that was in stark contrast to the aggressive hold of the sails. He reminisced about how similar the colors in the bay were to the hues and tones at the cottage and took note of how different and prehistoric the trees looked. A gliding seagull caught his eye, playfully positioned just higher than the mast. Dimitri continued to push the boat to exhilarating limits. The crash of a clamshell descending from the talons of a bird high above, hit the deck with a crack. Dimitri was faster to the shell than the gull; he worked the shell open for a quick briny snack.

"Lily, that gull is one of us, loves the water, always willing to share."

Under her sun scarf, Lily was quiet, just out of earshot. Dimitri steered the boat past a short beach just beyond the neighboring field. The seagull was still completely motionless alongside the boat. Lily was amazed at how far and how fast the seagull could travel without moving.

"With this wind at your back," Lily noted, "I bet you could outrun anyone, anywhere."

The boat and the bird remained in an inverted contest, one a whirlwind in constant motion, the other, still and aloft. Dimitri touched the boat with his whole body seemingly all at once. He reached for Lily.

"Come steer," he ordered.

The color of the shallow shoreline reflected the crisp combination of the sea and the sky.

He knew that if he swam ashore he could only stand on the beach for a short time. His sea legs needed to be maintained to pull himself faster and farther in between the chops and the breaks.

Just through the rocky channel, a million tiny ripples, not waves, welcomed them to the leeward side of Parker Cove. The evening was calm as they dropped anchor. Serene quiet fishing with long casts commenced. Lily took a moment to focus on their arrival, memorializing her daily entry into a sturdy leather journal. Three quaking aspen leaves were pressed deep into the parchment bringing the diary to life. She sensed their titillating rhythm, and the rapid motion of the leaves vibrating together in an otherwise isolated forest. With her eyes closed she imagined their solid bright golden color bursting to another dream, possessing an illuminating power. Holding the journal, it was as if she could see right through the pages, to the very essence of their meaning. The right frame followed. Her body seemed to hug the pages of the journal as she closed it. Her fingers tied the rustic leather cord into a unique knot she was certain only she could open.

The focused quality of light tightened in the moments following sunset. A welcome temperature change soothed the pair as they held each other closely. The latter half of a cool breeze hinted of the change of season that would soon arrive. Lily's half-asleep body leaned against Dimitri. He felt a quiver of a tickle on his chin as he moved closer to smell her perfumed hair. In a reflective moment he paused to count his tremendous blessings. The flicker and cadence of the small gentle waves reminded Dimitri of his favorite places; a boat almost in his name, and a cottage he shared with Stephen that seemed to be owned by a generous feline. He'd take either as long as Lily was with him.

As the sky grew darker, he felt the first twinkle of a lonely star, its neighbor arrived soon after. The brilliant orb and its bold companion welcomed the arrival of a deeper galaxy full of vibrant constellations. Dimitri was lost in the expansive black sky, mesmerized by the endless universe and the multitude of stars soaring high above them. Lily started to move slowly, her face resting on his shoulder. Their hands locked, relaxed, falling together in unison. When she looked up at him, a true reflection emanated from her eyes, her sparkled glance moved quickly past "find me" it urgently commanded, "come with me." Dimitri acted on the silent invitation lifting Lily to the padded platform and covering them both in a large blanket.

ABOUT THE AUTHOR

As a Deputy Chief of Staff and Legislative Aide, Realf Schermer has served as a trusted advisor to two State Senators. He began his writing journey crafting speeches, statements, and talking points shaping a career rooted in a deep passion for service. Realf has a love for the environment and the arts. He enjoys hiking on trail, learning how to play the guitar, and thinking creatively while writing or taking pictures. In his spare time, Realf enjoys the challenge of helping his children with their homework.

www.ingramcontent.com/pod-product-compliance
Lightning Source LLC
Chambersburg PA
CBHW020143120726
47903CB00007B/2397